"I don't date." Betsy's face flushed as she began to feel real anger at the way in which he was staring at her.

"How about a drink with me?" Nick asked.

"I told you, I don't want—"

He leaned down and kissed her, one hand moving over her breast. She could feel her nipple harden in response, sending electrical impulses through her body. She leaned against him, reaching up to encircle his neck with her arms, but he moved back, breaking off the kiss. His hand stayed on her breast, gently caressing it as he watched her reaction.

"Is this what you want?" he questioned.

She wanted all of him, wanted him so badly she could no longer reply. . . .

City Life, City Love

BEVERLY SOMMERS

A Love Affair from
HARLEQUIN
London · Toronto · New York · Sydney

First published in Great Britain in 1984
by Harlequin, 15–16 Brook's Mews, London W1A 1DR

ISBN 0 263 74628 3

18/0284

Made and printed in Great Britain by
Cox & Wyman Ltd, Reading

Chapter One

Betsy pushed the "execute" button on the keyboard, then watched with surprise as the document disappeared from the screen. *What now?* she wondered, having thought she had become proficient on the word processor by this time. She sent the machine to page one. The machine informed her she was already on page one. But that's not possible, she wanted to say to the machine, but had learned by now that errors were practically always hers. If what she was beginning to believe happened had happened in actuality, she had just deleted a sixty-page document. Gone. Effectively disappeared from the face of the earth. And yet she was sure she had known exactly what she was doing.

A temporary power failure? Possible. She looked around to see if the machine Christine was working on was not operating. No such luck. Christine was busily typing away, *her* document apparently alive and well and still on her screen.

The way she saw it she had two options. She could admit she lost the document—in which case she was in a lot of trouble—or she could try to retrieve it if, in fact, it was retrievable.

She canceled out and went back to the main menu, then once more pushed in her document number. It didn't flash "unknown document" at her, but a total blank came up on the screen. The same blank she had previously been looking at in disbelief. She sat back in her chair with a sigh. Perhaps it was nothing. It wouldn't be the first time she thought she had done something wrong, and each previous time one of the other word processors had put things right for her. It was just that now she wasn't training any longer, which meant that these things were no longer supposed to happen, and at the moment she was working on a very important document for one of the partners. To say nothing of the fact that she needed this job, and losing a sixty-page document could very well be cause for firing her.

She turned around. "Christine? Could you help me a minute?"

Always glad for an excuse to stop working, Christine bounced out of her chair and came over to see what the problem was.

"I seem to have lost my document," Betsy told her.

Christine looked at the blank screen. "Don't even say that, Betsy. How long was it?"

"Sixty pages."

"Is it on a disc?"

"No, I took it off to make the corrections."

Christine's expressive face took on a look of impending doom. "Well, I don't think they'll fire you—after all, it's happened to all of us at one time or another—but... who's document is it?"

"Mr. Creme's."

"Oh, dear. When it comes to work, Nicky can be a tyrant."

Until proven otherwise, Betsy considered them all potential tyrants. But those tyrants were her means of support at the moment. "What do I do, Christine, go in and tell him?"

Christine bestowed an angelic smile on her. "I'll go talk to him and smooth things over for you. I'll explain that you're new, inexperienced...He's not going to yell at *me*."

Betsy, who knew that the aspiring young actress had been dating Nick Creme, didn't think that was such a good idea. She had seen Christine in action more than once, batting her thickly mascaraed eyelashes, pouting her pretty little mouth, and in general taking on the demeanor of a little girl. No, she wasn't about to send a child to do a woman's work; she was perfectly prepared to admit her mistake to Mr. Creme and take the consequences herself.

"Thanks for the offer, Christine, but I'll do it. I feel terrible, though—it's the first time he's signed up for me." And probably the last, she thought wryly.

Betsy walked down the carpeted corridor where Nick Creme had a big corner office. She looked in, noting with relief that he was alone. Unlike Christine, she preferred performing without the benefit of an audience, and what she had to do could certainly be considered a performance.

Although the other night secretaries had kidded around with the lawyers and were on first-name terms with them, Betsy was not only new, but didn't really care to socialize on the job. She felt they were paying her very well, and for that salary she intended giving them a good night's work. Consequently, she had never exchanged a word with Nick Creme until he had handed her the work tonight, telling her it was imperative that it get done before she left.

He was seated at his desk and didn't hear her approach. She thought again, as she had thought the first time she had seen him, what an interesting-looking man he was. Unlike the other attorneys, most of whom had gone to Yale and still retained their preppie look, Nick Creme looked more like a longshoreman to her than a lawyer. An unruly head of dark hair worn rather long, a muscular body that never quite fit smoothly into his three-piece suits, and an olive complexion, the kind the other attorneys tried to get by using sunlamps, all combined to make him rather an anomaly in the firm, at least as far as looks went. Although the wire-rimmed glasses he currently wore perched on his nose seemed to give him a more serious look as befitted an expert tax attorney.

Well, she couldn't just stand there all night staring at him. "Mr. Creme?" she said, hoping her voice wouldn't betray her nervousness.

He looked up at her wordlessly, an annoyed look in his eyes.

"I'm sorry to have to tell you this, Mr. Creme..."

She had hoped maybe for a little prompting, but got no reaction at all.

"That document you gave me to correct..."

He raised one brow. "Is it finished?"

Betsy looked over his head and out the window,

the view of the Empire State Building, lit up in the distance, not even penetrating her mind. "No. It's gone."

The other brow joined the first. *"Gone?"*

Her eyes met his. "I deleted it."

She certainly had his full attention now. Two hands went up and managed to do more damage to an already disheveled head of hair. "You deleted an entire sixty-page document?" His tone was incredulous.

Her sentiments exactly. "Not intentionally," she hastened to add.

"I wouldn't imagine so." His tone implied that she had made a very silly remark.

Her eyes went past him again, but this time were disconcerted by her own image in the window. "I thought I was deleting two pages before making my insert, but the whole thing disappeared. I still don't know how it happened; one moment it was there, and the next..." Her voice trailed off as she realized she was making excuses when what she had done was really inexcusable.

He took off his glasses, placed them very carefully on the desk, then sunk his head in his hands with a groan. "Well, it's still on the disc, isn't it?"

He was more knowledgeable about the system than she had assumed the attorneys to be. "No, Mr. Creme. I had to take it off the disc to correct it." She watched him as he raised his head and lit a cigarette, throwing the match into an already overflowing ashtray. *He must be a very nervous man,* she surmised, hoping the cigarette might help to calm his nerves.

"Damn system ought to have some kind of fail-safe mechanism built into it," he muttered. "Well?" he said, surveying her through the smoke. "You realize I have to have that document first thing in the morning."

She nodded. "I'll start inputting it again now. I just wanted you to know it will probably be quite late by the time I finish it."

He looked at his watch.

She looked at hers and noted it was already past ten.

"If you're worried about overtime, I'll okay a voucher for you."

"I don't plan on putting in for overtime, Mr. Creme. If it hadn't been for my error, it wouldn't be needed."

He looked surprised, then a bit doubtful. "You better get started then, Ms.—"

"Miller. Betsy Miller." But he was already back at his work, effectively dismissing her.

Feeling warm, she stopped off at the washroom first to throw some cold water on her face. She looked pale, she thought, and it wasn't all due to the fluorescent lights in the bathroom. Her lipstick had all worn off during the course of the evening, and with her sandy-colored hair and fading tan, she looked all of a color, except for her green eyes. She also soaked her eyes with some water. They were already tired from staring at the word processing screen for several hours, though they no longer got bloodshot like when she first began to work there.

Christine looked up when Betsy got back to her work station. "What happened?"

Aware that the rest of the night staff found Nick Creme sexy, she had nonetheless come away with an impression of cold remoteness from the man. Since Christine was dating him, however, Betsy forced herself to smile and say lightly, "He was pretty nice about it."

"What are you going to do?"

"Start reinputting it, what else?" Betsy sat down in her chair and saw again the all-too-familiar blank screen.

"But that will take you all night!" wailed Christine, a stricken tone to her voice. "I'd stay and help you, but I've got an early audition tomorrow."

Betsy smiled her thanks at the offer. "Don't worry about it, Christine, it's my responsibility."

Someday I'll be so good on this machine, nothing *will ever go wrong,* Betsy vowed to herself as she began typing.

Around eleven, knowing she had at least three hours more of work ahead of her, she went to the kitchen to get a cup of coffee to help her stay alert. Susan and Lisa, looking like they were through for the night, were discussing a movie to be filmed in New York. Both of them were hoping to get work as extras. They had heard what had happened to her and offered their help, but Betsy turned it down. If it weren't for her own ineptness, she would be getting out early, too; she saw no reason for them to be penalized.

Awhile later George, the only male secretary on the

night staff and an aspiring chorus boy, came by to say good night, and since she hadn't seen Christine for a while, Betsy then assumed she was the last one there and would have to close down the system. It was an unusually quiet night for the lawyers; even the workaholics seemed to have left at a decent hour, although she was certain Nick Creme was still in his office, waiting for her to complete the document.

When she got to a word she couldn't decipher after numerous attempts, she carried the page down the hall to get it translated by Mr. Creme. Christine was in his office, decoratively draped across his desk, pouting aloud that "Nicky" didn't even have time for one little drink with her.

Betsy had almost decided not to interrupt when Nick saw her at the door and waved her inside. Christine, in a quick gesture, straightened out her skirt and sat up on the corner of the desk.

Feeling like an intruder, Betsy walked around the desk and pointed out the word to Mr. Creme.

"How's it coming?" he asked her.

"It'll be a while longer," she told him, sorry to be the cause of his canceling a date he might have had with Christine.

"Don't worry, I have plenty of work here to keep me busy," he assured her as she went out the door.

Back at her desk, Betsy thought about Christine and the others. She was the only member of the night staff not involved in the theater. She found the others friendly and quite entertaining, but when they occasionally asked her out with them for a drink after work, she always declined, which she was afraid was getting her the reputation of being antisocial. She felt she had little in common with them, though. None of them took the job seriously; it was just a means to an end, and each of them was convinced he or she would have made it on Broadway in no time at all, even though some of them had been trying now for years.

It was after two in the morning when Betsy finished the document and had run it off on the final printer. She ran off a second copy on the Xerox machine, then took them in to Mr. Creme.

He looked her over as she stood in front of his desk, not making any attempt to take the documents from her. "What is it about you? You seem different from the others," he finally said, but it didn't sound to her like a compliment.

She had hoped to blend into the office by wearing tailored blouses and straight skirts in dark colors, but instead was made to look conspicuous amidst the outrageous costumes the theater people tended to dress in. Even her sensible low-heeled shoes and her stockings looked strange among tights and brightly colored leg warmers.

Not knowing what to say, she simply shrugged, wishing he would take the documents so she could get out of there and go home.

He obviously hadn't had his say. "Are you an actress?"

"No." Only in New York, she thought, would a secretary have been asked that question.

He looked perplexed. "What are you?"

"A word processor," she replied, although after

her fiasco with the document, he could be justified in questioning *that*.

He leaned back in his chair and surveyed her through narrowed eyes. "Nothing else?"

It was actually none of his business, except he was one of the bosses, so she shook her head.

He was beginning to look genuinely intrigued. Good heavens, didn't they ever hire anyone but theater people? Did he consider her an impostor?

"Then why do you work nights?"

"I like working nights," she told him, which was the truth. Even if the circumstances were different, she might still look for a night job. She couldn't think of anything more delightful than being able to sleep in the morning as late as she liked.

"Doesn't that interfere with your social life?" he asked.

Now *that* was none of his business, she thought, but still she didn't want to make a bad impression. "I don't have a social life," she answered him honestly.

A corner of his mouth quirked. "Why not?"

She paused about ten seconds before answering, hoping he'd get the message that she no longer felt like being questioned on personal matters. After all, she had filled out the application in Personnel when applying for the job. And the questions he was asking her now would have been considered illegal on that same application; they would have been considered an invasion of privacy.

"I don't choose to," she finally said in a cool voice.

If he got the message, it had no effect on him. "You don't date?"

"No."

"Never?"

"Never." This was truly getting too personal, and she could feel her face flush as she began to feel real anger at the way in which he was interrogating her.

He gave her a condescending smile. "You're not going to catch a husband that way."

Betsy's green eyes took on a gleam. "I have no interest in *catching* a husband," she informed him sharply, taking extreme exception to his use of the word *catch*.

"That's what they all say," he observed blandly, a superior smile on his face.

Betsy's eyes now glowed with annoyance, and she had to stifle an urge to throw the documents in his face and wipe off that supercilious smile of his.

"Well, in my case, Mr. Creme, it's true. I think I can assure you that the *last* thing I want is a husband. I'd sooner catch...pneumonia!"

She was afraid she'd gone too far and that he would feel compelled to fire her on the spot for her impertinence, but instead he burst out laughing, his face suddenly looking years younger.

"Sorry," he said when he had stopped laughing. "We attorneys get into the habit of cross-examination, I'm afraid." He waved a hand toward his couch. "Just have a seat while I proof this, will you?"

Betsy settled down on the couch with a sigh, her anger slowly receding. She watched him for a moment as he slowly began to proofread the document. She had hoped she would be able to leave; now it looked as though there would be further corrections, and it would be the middle of the night before he excused her.

She glanced around the large corner office, not having actually seen anything but Mr. Creme up until now. Two walls were picture windows affording a marvelous view of lower Manhattan. The floor was carpeted luxuriously, almost indecently, in a dark green, and his desk was a slab of black marble on a chrome base—more table than desk.

She was vaguely wondering if he had decorated it himself, and then the next thing she knew, a hand was gently shaking her shoulder and she found she had been asleep. For a moment she thought she was home in bed, then she opened her eyes, ready to yell at being awakened so abruptly, and looked into the dark eyes of Nick Creme. She glanced at her watch and saw that it was now after three.

"You did an excellent job," he was telling her. "There are a few minor changes I still want to make, but nothing my secretary can't handle first thing in the morning. Why don't you shut down the system and call a cab?"

Betsy struggled up from the soft couch, blinking the sleep out of her eyes. "Are you sure you don't want me to do them?"

"Quite sure. Go home and get some sleep. And thank you for your help, Betsy."

She went around the offices, turning off machines and lights, then went into the room where the systems were housed and carefully turned them off the way she had been taught. She grabbed her tweed coat from the closet and was waiting for an elevator when Nick joined her.

She was afraid he would question her some more, but they rode down the eighteen floors of the Cranston Building in silence and were about to part on the sidewalk when he said, "I don't see your cab, would you like me to wait with you?"

"I always walk home," she informed him. "It's only ten blocks."

"You can't walk home alone at this hour," he said coldly.

Not wanting to get into an argument, she turned away, but was stopped by a firm hand on her shoulder. "You should know better than to walk around New York at night."

With a sigh, Betsy turned to face him. "I will never understand the combination of New Yorkers' paranoia and their refusal to live anywhere else. As long as I choose to live here I am not going to be intimidated to the point where I only feel safe in taxis."

She briefly noted the look of astonishment on his face, then turned away from him, once more to be seized by the shoulder and halted in her tracks.

"Paranoia?" His voice sounded strangled.

She turned back to him. "Yes—paranoia."

"Practically everyone I know's been mugged at least once. You call that paranoia?"

"I haven't been mugged, and I walk home alone every night."

"Then you must be new to the city—your turn will come."

"Look, Mr. Creme, it's just down Lexington Avenue. It's perfectly safe," she explained patiently, wishing he would let go of her so that she could get home to bed.

"You're a nut, you know that?"

Her eyes flashed. "But not a *paranoid* one!"

"All the other night workers take cabs home. I'm sure you were told the company pays for it."

"But they all live quite a distance from work. One of the reasons I took this job, Mr. Creme, was so that I could walk to work. I like the exercise."

"You can share a cab with me," he said, his voice a veritable growl.

"I don't *want* to share a cab with you." She had *never* met a more exasperating man.

"I assure you *I* don't pose any threat to you." He was already waving down a taxi, and seconds later holding the door open for her.

With a sigh of annoyance not lost on him, she decided she had better give in and let him have his way, otherwise she'd probably never get home. She got into the cab and settled into the backseat, telling the driver to drop her off at Lexington and Thirty-second Street.

Nick sat down beside her, his bulk squeezing against her. "Do you live on the corner?" he asked.

She moved as far away from him as she could, ending up practically hugging the door. She thought she heard him chuckle as she moved, but might have been imagining it.

"No," she told him, "but I only live a few doors in, and Thirty-second runs east."

"The driver can go around the block." The tone of his voice had a certain finality to it.

"It's a very safe block," she said in a mutinous voice.

"No block is safe at this hour."

She had a sudden urge to scream *"PARANOID"* at the top of her lungs, and just the thought of doing it made her feel better. *Good heavens,* she thought, *how does he think I survive the rest of the time?* She stared out the window while he instructed the driver during the short drive to her building.

"Thank you," she muttered when they arrived, getting quickly out of the cab, then saw with disbelief that he was joining her.

"This isn't necessary," she said as he stood by the door while she searched for her keys in her handbag.

"You should have your keys in your hand by the time you get out of a taxi," he instructed her in a smug voice.

"Along with my whistle and my can of Mace, right?"

"I'll overlook the sarcasm—"

"You don't *have* to overlook it, it was *intentional*." She flared out at him, momentarily forgetting she was dependent on him for her employment. She hung her head in what she hoped looked like a contrite manner. "I apologize, Mr. Creme, but it's late, and I'm very tired. Thank you for the ride home, thank you for seeing me to my door..." She couldn't think of anything else to thank him for.

She looked up at him. It was too dark to see the expression on his face, but she was sure it wasn't a pleasant sight.

"I realize you find it amusing, but if something had happened to you, I would have felt responsible." He took the keys from her hand and quickly opened the outer door, then handed them to her.

"I could just as easily get mugged *going* to work," she felt impelled to point out to him.

"Going to work is *your* responsibility," he said in a steely voice, then bade her good night and returned to the taxi, where the driver had been following the exchange with some enjoyment.

Betsy climbed the three flights to her apartment, then turned to knock softly on the other door on the landing.

A sleepy Abby opened the door, looking tiny and childlike in her flannel nightgown, her long dark hair hanging down her back. "Why are you so late?"

"I'll tell you about it in the morning," said Betsy. "Get back to bed. I'll let myself out."

Abby did as she was told, and Betsy went over to the couch and lifted Jason from beneath the blanket. He slowly slid from her arms to his feet, and she led him, half asleep, out of the apartment and into their own, where he quickly crawled beneath the covers of his trundle bed. "Good night, Mom," he murmured, then went immediately back to sleep.

Betsy knew she was too keyed-up from the argument with Mr. Creme to get right to sleep, so she put the kettle on for some hot chocolate. While it was boiling she made the couch into her bed and then got into her own flannel nightgown. Only no one could accuse her of looking like a child, she thought ruefully, noting her ample curves. She wasn't fat, but she could stand to lose a few pounds, she thought as she looked at herself in the mirror behind the bathroom door. Or maybe it was just that she was suddenly working with young women who dieted themselves to skin and bones because the camera put on pounds. As for Abby, her nervous energy kept her slim. Well, she wasn't out to land a television commercial, nor was she, as Mr. Creme had so aptly put it, trying to catch a husband, so she guessed she'd just live with herself the way she was.

She fixed the hot chocolate, then settled herself in bed, the latest thriller by Robert Ludlum open in front of her. But the book didn't seem to hold her interest tonight. She thought of how close she had come to perhaps being fired, and repressed a shudder. She didn't want anything to interfere with the perfect arrangement she and Abby had worked out. It would have been enough just to make such a good friend as her neighbor, with the added bonus that Abby's daughter, Carla, was only a few months older than Jason, which gave him someone to play with in the building. As Betsy had found out, there weren't too many children living in her neighborhood—and Jason would have been very lonely if it weren't for Carla. But Abby was more than just a neighbor. She had told Betsy about the law firm where she worked days, and it had been partially her recommendation that had gotten Betsy the night job there. Which left Betsy free to supervise the kids during the day, and

Abby to watch them at night—an arrangement that made it possible for them to live on their salaries. With the added cost of baby-sitters, it would have proved very difficult.

Betsy had been so confident of being able to get a job when she had told her husband, a husband in the process of leaving her, that she was remaining in New York with Jason. "I can always type," she had informed him, not knowing that in the interim during which she had been married, most of the offices were converting to word processors, which made her skills practically obsolete. But the law office had been willing to train her, and once trained, the money was far better than she would have received as a typist. She also found the machine both a challenge and fun to operate—when she wasn't deleting entire documents, that is.

She also couldn't have asked for a better friend than Abby. Totally different in temperament, the two of them hit it off from the start. Betsy's usual calm, practical manner was the perfect foil for Abby's volatile personality, and each enjoyed the contrast. Divorced also, Abby was in perfect agreement with Betsy as far as "never again" when it came to marriage, and they were both determined they could bring up their children better alone than with the presence of a man around.

When she thought about it, Betsy couldn't really blame Nick Creme for his assumption that the secretaries were all looking for husbands. She had to admit it certainly seemed to be true of the others. The actresses she worked with were all constantly on the lookout for a man to support them, with or without the benefit of matrimony, thus freeing them for auditions and rehearsals and classes and all other matters that make up aspiring actresses' lives. And an attorney would be a likely proposition. Several of the attorneys were divorced, there were a few young bachelors, and all of them had the means of supporting a wife in style. She had noticed that most of them seemed flattered by the attention they received from the pretty young thespians.

She had, in fact, heard Mr. Creme was divorced, but couldn't remember any of the details. At the time she had gotten all the attorneys mixed up, and it was only lately that she had been able to put faces to names—not that she was interested in his marital status. She only hoped Christine wasn't foolish enough to pursue one of the married attorneys.

She remembered the look of surprise on her husband's face when she told him she was remaining in New York. And Tom had had a right to look shocked, because ever since his transfer to the city, she had done nothing but complain. After finally buying the house of their dreams in a northern Chicago suburb, a lovely two-story home on half an acre of property, which she had carefully and lovingly furnished, decorated, and landscaped, he had told her that not only was he being transferred to New York City, but he had specifically *requested* the transfer. Betsy had felt her secure, familiar world crashing around her. Their friends were all in Glenview, Jason's very good school was there, and they had recently been accepted as members into the local country club, where she was taking tennis lessons three times a week. All of her happiness seemed to be bound up within the confines of that lovely town.

She argued with Tom to no avail. It was a promotion, and nothing she said could convince him to turn it down once having succeeded in getting it. Resigned to the inevitable, she had flown to New York to look for a cooperative apartment and found that what they could afford turned out to be a small two-bedroom on the Upper East Side. The rooms were tiny and dark, the windows looked out onto other windows, there was no washer or dryer—not even a dishwasher. The closets were inadequate, the floors bare of carpeting, and a tenacious colony of roaches had settled in for a long stay. Then Tom insisted that Jason attend a private school so he wouldn't pick up any nasty habits, such as a New York accent or the use of a switchblade, the consequences of which was that for the first time they were living beyond their means.

It was with a heavy heart that Betsy watched their house and much of its contents being sold. She had a farewell party for their friends, then she boarded the plane with Tom, a tearful Jason in their wake.

And then, after only two months in New York, Tom broke the news. He had been conducting an affair back in Glenview with a neighbor of theirs, and he now found that he couldn't live without her. He not only wanted a divorce, he was transferring back to the Chicago office.

Betsy, who had thought there could be no more surprises in store for her, found herself taking this much more calmly than she had taken the move. She was brokenhearted at Tom's betrayal of her, at the breakup of their marriage, which she thought had been near perfect, but she refused to let him see it and conducted all their prebreakup discussions with a stoicism that seemed to puzzle him. She was adamant on two points: she didn't want any alimony or child support from him—she wanted him to sever himself completely from them. And two, she refused to move back to Glenview with Jason. Despite Tom's pleading and the fact that Jason would rarely be able to see his father, Betsy would not return to the scene of the crime, so to speak, and refused to be drawn back into a social life where Tom and his new wife would always be present.

They sold their furnished co-op, and Betsy took half the money from the sale as her "community property." She didn't really want to take it, but she knew she would need it to keep Jason and herself while she found an apartment and a job. She found the small apartment in Murray Hill and installed Jason in a nearby public school, which delighted the child, as he had hated the strict private school he had been attending. It was true that the entire apartment could have fit into their master bedroom in Glenview, but she found she was quite happy there. Far happier, in fact, than she had ever been in the co-op. It was bright and sunny, facing out over a view of roof gardens. She painted the walls white, had the wood floors refinished, and furnished it with practical butcher-block-type furniture that couldn't be damaged by an active boy. Despite Jason's pleadings, she refused to buy a TV set, but since he could watch TV at Abby's, he wasn't really deprived. As she explained to him, she would only be able to watch it days, and she wasn't about to start watching soap operas. Instead she installed bookshelves and started a growing collection of paperbacks.

She was determined to build a completely new life for herself—totally different from the suburban one she had led before. Exactly what that life would encompass she hadn't had time to think about yet, but she knew that eventually she should probably return to school and prepare herself for some kind of a career. That would take some thinking, though, as she had never thought in terms of a career before, and the possibilities were overwhelming.

Right now she was content just to have found a job and to be able to support herself and Jason, if not in luxury, at least adequately. And, as she had told Nick Creme, another husband was the last thing she wanted. When you could live with someone for ten years and love him, and then have it turn out that you didn't know him at all—well, that was something she was never going to risk having happen again. Besides, she found she liked being self-sufficient; it was particularly nice not having to ask Tom for money or having to justify every dollar she spent. For the first time in her life she felt like a real adult.

And yet, in some inexplicable way, she felt young in the city. She was no longer a suburban housewife but a working woman, part of that vast throng of smartly clad young women who filled the subways and buses during rush hours. With no large house to clean, no yard work, no car pools, and no social engagements, even while working she found she had more time to herself than ever before. Days, while Carla and Jason were in school, she could explore the city at her leisure, visiting museums and art galleries, and she had even sat in on UN sessions on occasion, it being only a short walk from her apartment. She also found she very much enjoyed Jason's company, and the boy didn't have to plead with his mother to spend time with him on weekends. And instead of the women she saw socially being the wives of Tom's business friends, she had Abby, the closest friend she had had since her school days.

She did sometimes long for a room of her own, but the tiny one-bedroom apartment had been all she could afford. She had originally intended taking the bedroom herself, but after viewing Jason's five hundred comic books, his bat and ball and glove, his football, his skateboard, his roller skates, and about a hundred other precious possessions of his that he couldn't be persuaded to part with, she finally conceded that he needed the room more than she did. All she had were a few suitable clothes she had purchased for work, and a lot of unsuitable clothes, like tennis outfits and evening dresses, that she had packed away in cartons and put on top of the closet shelf.

It was very late when she finally turned out the lamp and crawled under the covers, but she knew she'd be able to take a nap the following day while the children were in school. She thought briefly of the cool Mr. Creme, obviously used to having his orders obeyed, if the taxi ride was any indication, and wondered what it was that Christine saw in him. He must be at least thirty-five, and Christine couldn't be much more than twenty-two and certainly no match for his domineering manner. And yet she imagined that was probably what thirty-five-year-olds wanted—sweet young girls they could dominate completely, thus reinforcing the macho image most men seemed to think was necessary. At least Tom had not been *that* foolish.

Well, that type certainly wasn't for her. Not that any type was anymore. She had enjoyed her marriage and certainly hadn't wanted a divorce, but now that she'd tasted the joys of single life, she was determined never to give them up again.

Chapter Two

"So Nick brought you home in a taxi?"

Betsy and Abby were having a cup of coffee together in Abby's kitchen while the children got themselves dressed for school.

"Under duress," Betsy pointed out emphatically.

"But still... if word got around, you two would be an item."

"Oh, come on, Abby—a *taxi* ride?"

"A taxi ride with Nick Creme is tantamount to—"

"An affair?"

Abby gave her a wicked look. "Let's say a... brief encounter."

"In other words, a one-night stand." Betsy believed in calling a spade a spade.

"Umm, you have the picture."

"Well, I'm sure he wouldn't want the word to get around. At the moment he's dating Christine."

Abby lighted a cigarette and inhaled deeply, a look of pure pleasure on her face. "Oh, yes. And Barbara Walton and Jeanne Brunda and Claudia Daitch."

"He's dating *all* of them?"

"I don't know about *dating*; I know he's *seeing* all of them." Her dark eyes positively danced. "And those are just the ones in the office. His secretary says unknown women, at least unknown to her, call him all day on the phone and leave plaintive messages for him.''

Betsy helped herself to another wide wedge of the pecan ring sitting on the table. ''I hate men like that,'' she muttered.

''Oh, Nick's not so bad. He's just out to prove something since his wife left him, that's all. Kind of like what you're doing, only in reverse.''

Betsy chose to ignore the last part. ''What's he trying to prove, that he's God's gift to women?''

Abby chuckled. ''Well, a lot of women seem to think he is. You really can't argue with success. And, as I was saying, you're doing the same thing in reverse. You could probably have just about any man you wanted, but you're nasty to them all.''

''*Nasty?* I'm not nasty.''

''How about Tony?''

Betsy burst out laughing. ''The *super*?''

''Well, he was coming on pretty strong to you.''

''The *super*?'' she repeated.

''Well, if you had been nicer to him, we might have gotten a monthly exterminator out of him.''

''I wasn't nasty to him. I just wasn't interested.''

''*And* the men at the office. You know how much gossip there is around there. I don't know what you've said to them, but I hear tell the men think you're frigid.'' She smiled while that information sunk in.

''Abby, I don't even know most of their names yet. I just do my work and go home.''

Abby seemed about to say something else when the bathroom door opened and Carla emerged, wearing a frilly pink creation that would have been suitable attire for a flower girl in a wedding.

Abby looked her over casually. "Lovely, darling. Now go change into your school clothes."

Carla gave her mother a deceptively innocent look. "But you said it makes me look like a fairy princess."

"Exactly. Now go change."

Carla's lower lip stuck out in defiance. "Magda gets to wear—"

"Magda is a gypsy; you're not."

"Well, I'd *like* to be a gypsy."

"When you're eighteen you can be anything you like. Until then..."

With a flounce of her skirts Carla went back into the bathroom and slammed the door.

"At times I'd like to give her to the gypsies," Abby murmured.

"They have gypsies at their school?" Betsy asked with interest.

"As far as I know, just Magda. Her mother's the one with the fortune-telling shop over the deli."

Jason came into the apartment more suitably attired and sidled up to his mother. "Can we go to the park Saturday?"

"Did you get your homework done?"

He nodded. "Can we go to the park Saturday?"

"Jason, it's only Wednesday."

"But I want to *know*."

"Don't we always go to the park on Saturdays?"

He nodded happily.

Abby looked from one to the other. "You two

should be in commercials,'' she said, not for the first time. ''I mean it, Betsy. You look identical, and you both have that happy All-American look the sponsors seem to love so much.''

Betsy looked at Jason. With his sandy hair cut short and curling around his face, his long-lashed green eyes, small turned-up nose with a sprinkling of freckles across it, and even the same wide mouth, it was like looking at a mirror image of herself, albeit younger. Then he smiled, revealing his gap-toothed grin, and the resemblance ended.

Carla finally appeared in jeans and a blue sweater, and the two women put on their coats to leave. They parted at the corner, Abby to walk uptown to work, and Betsy to walk the children the few blocks downtown to school. She realized that where she had no paranoia concerning her own safety, she *was* more careful about Jason's safety in the city than she would have been back in Glenview, where he had been allowed to ride his bike to school.

When they got to the entrance of the building, Jason hung his head and mumbled, ''Don't kiss me, Mom.''

Betsy smiled down at him. ''No kiss good-bye?''

He shook his head. ''The other kids will make fun of me.''

Betsy gave him a pat on the shoulder instead, thinking how quickly he was growing up, said good-bye to Carla, then headed back to her apartment. There was an interesting Middle-Eastern crisis going on, and she had thought of spending the morning sitting in on the meeting of the Security Council at the

UN, but the few hours sleep she had gotten weren't proving adequate. Instead she went back to bed and slept until past noon.

She picked up the kids after school and took them to the library over on Third Avenue, where they were each allowed to choose two books, and she was able to find an armful for herself, then took them home and settled them down with fruit juice and cookies while she began to get ready for work.

She took a shower and washed her hair, blowing it dry quickly, then spent more time on makeup than she usually did. Nothing spectacular, just a little blush and some brown mascara, as the fluorescent lights really did make everyone look washed out.

When Abby arrived she was ready to go.

"Did you take a nap?" Abby wanted to know.

"Umm, a few hours." She felt rather decadent at having slept away half the day.

Abby laughed. "Well, obviously Nick didn't—he was like a bear all day. And I hate to be the bearer of bad tidings, no pun intended, but I looked in the night book when I signed out, and he's got you booked again."

Betsy's eyes widened. "Why? How could he possibly want me to work for him after I deleted his entire document?"

"Well, now, knowing Nick, he's got to see you as a challenge."

"A *challenge*?"

"You as much as told him you weren't interested in men, which to someone like Nick would mean a personal affront. Yes, I think he'd take that as a challenge.''

Betsy surveyed herself in the mirror as she put on her coat. "Tell me the truth, Abby, do I dress too conservatively for the office?"

Abby appraised the oxford-cloth shirt in beige, the brown tweed skirt and matching coat, the smoothly stockinged legs, the low-heeled leather shoes with crepe soles and shook her head. "No, you look very professional. The way secretaries *used* to look."

"The rest of the night staff all dress so. . .exotically."

"Yes, I sometimes see them coming in when I'm leaving. The day secretaries seem to be evenly divided between the married ones, who wear jeans, and the unmarried ones, who dress more like cocktail waitresses. Don't worry about it—the female attorneys all dress like you, and they're the successful ones."

Betsy buttoned up her coat and turned to go.

"Don't let Nick keep you out too late tonight," was Abby's parting advice, said in a teasing tone.

Betsy grinned in amusement. "Don't worry. Anyway, I want to catch the session at the UN in the morning."

"You and the UN. Don't you find it boring?"

Betsy shook her head. "The whole time I was married I wasn't even aware there was a world out there. Now that I am, I find it endlessly fascinating."

"You should stick to soap operas, they're safer."

"Well, I'll keep you posted on the continuing saga of *One Life to Live*, according to the doctrine of Nicholas Creme."

She walked along Lexington, buffeting the crowds of office workers leaving for the day, heading in the direction of Forty-second. The closer she got to Grand Central Station and the Cranston Building, the more hectic it became. There was a cacophony that nearly numbed her mind: shouts, curses, the bleat of horns, the squeal of brakes, sirens, bells, whistles, the blast of punk rock from the open doors of music shops, and the demanding cries of street vendors and beggars. It was a hurly-burly that simply swept her up and carried her along until she found herself trotting, dashing through traffic against the lights, shouldering her way through the press, rushing, rushing— senseless and invigorating.

She wondered why Nick had again signed up for her; then, when she signed in, she noticed it was Christine's night off and thought that must be the reason.

She was a bit on edge in preparation for another encounter with him, but he had left her work in the night staff's basket and gone for the day. The night went quickly, if uneventfully, and she and the others were out of there by eleven thirty.

ON THURSDAY, though, Nick had again signed up for her, and this time Christine was there, looking fetching in powder-blue leotard and tights, a filmy dance skirt over the outfit. The young actress told Betsy confidentially that Nick had decided to use Betsy at night from then on.

"But why? I would think after what I did he'd *never* want to use me again."

"He says you have a businesslike attitude and do good work," Christine explained softly. "Also, he says I'm entirely too sexy and it distracts him." She giggled, tossing her long hair back from her piquant face.

"I hope you don't mind, Christine—I know you always worked for him."

"Don't worry, Betsy, I don't mind at all—his work's *boring*! Anyway, it's probably not too good to mix business and pleasure, if you know what I mean. I'm working on the litigation side tonight, and that's much more interesting."

That night Nick Creme worked late in his office, but except for thanking Betsy when she handed him the work, they didn't speak at all. *I was all primed for battle,* Betsy thought ruefully, *and there wasn't even a skirmish.*

FRIDAY NIGHT was a slow night for work, which was just as well, as Christine had called in sick, Lisa had taken the night off to appear in a play reading, and Susan was off regularly on Fridays. That left just Betsy and George to divide up the work.

At eleven, just when they thought they were finished for the night, Nick appeared and asked if one of them would mind doing a tape for him.

Betsy could see George's stricken eyes on her and she was aware he had a date after work. "I'll do it, Mr. Creme," she said, holding out her hand for the tape.

"Thanks, Betsy," George breathed, then rushed out of the office before someone else appeared with work.

Nick gave a slight smile. "I didn't figure George would volunteer."

"George has a social life," she couldn't resist saying.

The smile widened. "Unlike you."

"Exactly." She put the tape in the Dictaphone and popped on the headset before he could come back with some retort.

An hour later when she handed him the transcribed tape, he looked up at her from behind his desk.

"You don't work Saturdays, do you?"

"No, Mr. Creme."

"I was wondering if you'd mind coming in for an hour in the morning. I wouldn't ask, but everyone's booked up for tomorrow, and I have to have this by noon to drop off at a client's office. I thought since you lived so close..."

She thought quickly. "I'd be glad to stay tonight and do it."

"And risk another argument with you over a cab?"

She managed to control the laughter welling up in her at the reference to Wednesday night's fiasco.

"It's got to be tomorrow," he said. "It'll take me a couple of hours to revise it, and there's no sense in your just sitting around here waiting."

"What time would you want me?"

He shrugged. "That's up to you."

"What if I come in at ten thirty?"

"That would be fine. It might not even take you an hour. You're a fast typist, I've noticed."

Which probably makes up for my big mouth, Betsy mused.

She shut down the machines, thinking that if she was out of there the next morning by eleven thirty, that would still give her and Jason most of the day together in the park. And the amount of overtime she would make would just pay for a nice dinner out for them Saturday night. Not Jason's choice this time, she was getting sick of McDonald's, but maybe the Indian restaurant she walked past on Lexington when she took them to school. Jason would complain at first about the unfamiliarity of the food, but he always ended up eating everything in sight. Rather like her, in that respect.

THE NEXT MORNING there was a chill in the air, and she could hear the radiators clanging away as she got out of bed. The radio said the temperature had dropped to the thirties, and in addition to her coat she got out a muffler and gloves to wear to work. Jason, happy to spend Saturday morning watching cartoons with Carla, didn't complain when she told him she had to go in to the office for an hour, and just told her to be back in time for the park.

"Ummm, a weekend assignation with the indomitable Mr. Creme," mused Abby when Betsy dropped Jason off.

"Just a quick hour's typing. And because of the overtime I'm treating us to Indian food tonight."

Abby's face brightened. "Sounds good. I think we'll join you."

"I'm not eating Indian food," protested Carla, who had no trouble following the cartoons and her mother's conversation simultaneously.

"Of course you are—it's what gypsies eat," Abby informed her, with a wink at Betsy.

"Oh...okay," came from the direction of the TV.

Outside, the sky was hard, an icy blue whitened by a blurry sun, and in the west a faded wedge of morning moon. Not a cloud. But an angry wind came steadily and swirled the streets. Betsy found she had to duck her head to keep her eyes from watering. It was almost November and looked like it was going to be an early winter.

When Betsy arrived at the office, face glowing from the cold, she was surprised to find everyone but herself in casual dress, including the attorneys. Dignified Mr. Beckwith was even wearing a bright red running suit. She thought if it weren't for spending the day with Jason, it might be fun working Saturdays.

Nick, wearing skintight jeans and a black sweat shirt with a picture of Mozart adorning it, was in the kitchen, drinking coffee and reading the paper, when she tracked him down.

Now he does *look like a longshoreman,* she thought with amusement as he looked up at her.

"Something funny?" he asked.

"No. I just didn't realize everyone dressed so casually on weekends."

"Did you think we wore our business suits to bed at night?" he asked gruffly.

"I was sure *you* didn't," she said sweetly, then flushed when she realized how personal her remark sounded.

But he was laughing. "You like putting me in my place, don't you?"

Betsy just shook her head, biting her lip to keep from laughing.

"It's all right, my ego can take it."

Then she *did* burst out laughing, hanging on to the edge of the table for support. She was equally sure his ego could take it; it was probably of the largest proportions she had ever witnessed.

"What's so funny? You think I have a big ego?"

"I don't even know you, Mr. Creme," she managed to gasp through her laughter.

"That's true. You don't. Not yet."

He reached into the briefcase by his chair and brought out the document she had typed the night before. "If you could get serious for a minute..."

He waited patiently while her laughter wore down, then, as she was wiping her eyes with her sleeve, he said, "This shouldn't take you too long. There weren't as many corrections as I had anticipated. I'll need an original and two copies."

She took the pages and nodded, not yet trusting herself to speak. He was once again reading the morning *Times* as she left the kitchen.

Forty-five minutes later she found him in his office and handed him the document.

He quickly glanced through the original. "Did you proof it?"

"Of course."

He raised a brow. "Not everyone does."

She was surprised to hear that, as proofing had been something that was stressed during her training.

"It looks very nice. Thank you. I appreciate your giving up your Saturday morning to come in."

She wondered briefly if he would have asked it of someone who had a social life. "You're welcome, Mr. Creme," she murmured, then turned to leave.

A gruff voice stopped her. "You're something of an enigma in this office, you know that?"

Betsy turned around, a puzzled look on her face. "An *enigma*?"

"Yes, a...puzzle."

"I understand what the word means," she informed him. "I just don't understand why you think *I'm* one."

"Well, for one thing, you don't...flirt."

She guessed that *was* unusual for this office. "You have to be interested to flirt," she informed him coolly and saw the instant look of challenge come into his eyes. She had done it again—quite unintentionally stirred up his interest just when she wanted to get out of there and go home.

He looked at his watch, then eyed her speculatively. "How about having a drink with me?"

"I thought you had to deliver that to a client."

"I can send it over by messenger."

She sighed. "I told you I don't—"

He raised his hands. "It's not a date, I swear. Just consider it a drink with a colleague."

Her green eyes narrowed. "It *sounds* like a date." *And I don't consider you a colleague,* she added to herself.

"It's not—it's just a drink. It's *daylight* out."

She looked past him out the window as if to confirm what he said. "Thank you, Mr. Creme, but I'd rather not."

She watched him as he ran his hands through his shaggy hair, a bemused expression on his face.

"Could you at least call me Nick? We're very informal here, you know."

She supposed she could concede him *that*. "If you don't need me any longer, Nick..."

"No, you can go. But Betsy..."

"Yes?"

"When I was prosecuting cases for the Internal Revenue Service—"

"You were with the *IRS*?"

"Yes. Anyway—"

"I *hate* the IRS!"

"You're *supposed* to hate the IRS. It instills fear. That way you pay your taxes. Anyway, as I was saying..." He paused as though waiting for her to interrupt again. When she didn't, he continued. "When I was prosecuting cases for the IRS...I never lost a case." He paused for the full effect. When she showed no reaction he looked annoyed. "Do you get what I'm driving at?"

"No."

"What that means is, I always succeed in what I set out to do."

"*I* think it means simply that you can't beat the government," Betsy said with an impish grin, then turned and left his office.

JASON WAS WAITING IMPATIENTLY when she got home, dressed and ready to go in worn jeans, sneakers, and his Windbreaker.

"It's gotten cold out, Jason. I think you better wear something warmer."

"Can I wear my new down jacket?" It had writing on the back. Jason *only* liked clothes that had writing on them.

She thought of the rough treatment it might get in the park. But he would be warm in it. "Sure, honey. I'll be ready in just a minute."

She changed into her worn jeans, a sweat shirt, and running shoes and put on her new down vest, the same bright color of red as Jason's jacket, only sans writing. Unlike Jason, and some other people she could think of, she didn't care for advertising to appear on her clothes, in either pictures or writing. After Betsy pulled a matching red knit cap down over her ears, they set out for the park.

So far Betsy's two favorite things about the city were walking—which she planned to do now, as the park was only a mile and a half away—and Central Park itself. She had heard horrors about the place, of course, and she imagined Nick Creme would be equally paranoid about her going in there as he was about her walking home alone at night, but she found the place an absolute delight. Already she and Jason had been to the zoo several times, had taken a rowboat out in the lake, had rented bicycles and ridden down the park's paths, and she was looking forward to ice-skating there in the winter. During the summer she and Abby had taken the children to the free concerts and opera in the park. The children hadn't been so thrilled about that, far preferring to watch TV, but she liked the fact that Jason was getting some culture, something he never received in Glenview.

They walked up Fifth Avenue, skirting the people

who were crowding into the stores. They had a large pretzel on Forty-sixth Street, and Cokes on Fifty-ninth at the entrance to the park. They walked along the paths filled with joggers and cyclists and people walking their dogs. The benches were filled with people feeding the pigeons and themselves, and an occasional game of chess was being played by the old men. Couples were wheeling babies and small children in carriages and strollers, and many lovers, of all combinations of sexes, were strolling along hand in hand.

With no particular destination in mind, they strolled into the interior of the park, pausing occasionally to pet a dog or get a drink from a water fountain. Jason spotted a football game in progress. It seemed to be made up of boys from around eight to fourteen. He hung around watching until Betsy gave him a little shove and told him he could go join them.

"But what will you do, Mom?"

"Don't worry about me. I'll just watch you for a while."

Jason ran into the throng of boys and was quickly assimilated into their game. Betsy stood leaning against a tree, watching. She had been the only girl in a family of boys and, as a child, had played many a game of football with her brothers. As she watched she felt restless, itchy. *You're too old for that, my girl,* she derided herself silently. *And your son would not appreciate his big lump of a mother nosing in on his game.*

She decided to do a little jogging up and down the

length of the playing field. It wouldn't hurt to lose
some of the flab, she told herself; get in shape like the
actresses she worked with. Not that she'd ever be *that*
thin, she just wasn't built that way. She was afraid
that no matter how much weight she lost she'd still
have hips and more than a discernible bust.

One of the boy's kicks went awry and she saw the
ball heading in her direction. With a swift and graceful
movement, she scooped it up and fired it to Jason. *A
perfect pass,* she thought to herself; *I've still got it!*

She noticed that Jason had caught the ball and was
standing there looking at her with his mouth hanging
open. Acting totally unconcerned, she dug the toe of
her shoe into the grass and watched out of the corner
of her eye as the boys on Jason's team went into a
huddle and then casually approached her as a group.

"You wanna be our quarterback, lady?" one of
the older boys asked her.

She shrugged, trying to look cool.

"You could kick the extra points, too."

That was inducement beyond her wildest dreams.
Her brothers had never let her kick the extra points.

Without a word Betsy trotted onto the field and
drew her team into a huddle. She told them exactly
what she wanted them to do, then the team took up
its positions.

"One, four, seven, eight—hike!" she yelled, then
caught the ball and dropped back to make a pass. She
had plenty of time, as she was getting excellent cover-
age. As she moved around she saw out of the corner of
her eye a small crowd gathering to watch the game.

She finally got the pass off, a real beauty, and she

yelled with delight when the receiver took it all the way down the field for a touchdown. She kicked an impressive extra point, and then it was the other team's chance at the ball.

She looked over at the crowd of people and could have sworn she saw Nick Creme's shaggy head among them. *Now you* are *getting paranoid,* she scolded herself. Nick Creme at her football game would be just too much of a coincidence.

On the first play the other team fumbled the ball, and once again Betsy was going to get a chance to pass. This time, however, as soon as she dropped back with the ball, she could have sworn she heard someone shout, "Atta way, Betsy!" and when she looked around to see who said that, eight boys ran into her, sent her sprawling, then jumped on top of her. That aspect of football had somehow escaped her memory.

When she had extricated herself from the pile of warm bodies, she looked over at the crowd once more but didn't see a familiar face. And if it had been Nick, he would certainly have waited to see her demoralized expression after goofing that last play so disastrously.

The game lasted for a couple of hours, and when it was over the boys told them both to be sure and return the following Saturday.

"You're our secret weapon, lady," one of the kids said to her with respect in his eyes.

Jason was beside himself with awe on the way home. "Gee, Mom, you play football just like a boy," he kept saying to her. Doing anything "like a boy'' was the highest accolade Jason could bestow on her. In the past he had told her she ran like a boy and, once, when they were playing catch, that she threw like a boy, but it seemed that playing football like a boy was an even worthier feat.

All through dinner at the Indian restaurant Abby and Carla were treated to verbal instant replays of the football game.

"I didn't know you had such hidden talents," Abby finally said with a raised brow.

With enough quarters to keep the children occupied at the arcade games for a while, Betsy related the morning's conversation with Nick.

"Score one for us old ladies against those sweet young things," said Abby, grinning.

"As you pointed out, Abby, I think he just considers me a challenge."

"Yes, but that could be heady stuff for a guy who has women flinging themselves at him."

"I suppose I should try flinging *myself* and put an end to this nonsense."

"That's not your style."

"No. I never did act like that with men, even when I was interested in them."

"He wouldn't be a bad catch, Betsy."

"Oh, no—now you sound just like him!"

"He's single, good-looking, sexy, intelligent—and he makes a good living."

"And you could be describing my ex-husband."

"Well, you were satisfied with him."

Betsy grimaced. "If you want him, Abby, *you* go after him."

"It's not *me* he finds intriguing."

"We've got to cut this out, Abby. Do you realize we're talking about men? We never used to talk about men."

"You're right—I lost my head. But it's not as though it's like how we used to be, in our youth. I think tearing down an obvious sex symbol like Nick Creme is really progress."

"Does this mean we're liberated at last, Abby?"

"It sure as hell does, honey."

"But he *is* sexy, I'll grant you that," Betsy had to admit.

"Damn right he is."

"Poor man. He's not going to get his way this time."

"I wouldn't lay odds on it," said Abby wryly.

When they got home Abby invited Betsy and Jason in to watch TV, but Betsy declined.

"One hour only, Jason," she told him when he began his deprived child act, then she got into a hot tub to try to soothe her already aching muscles. Football used a lot more muscles than walking, she decided with a groan, knowing she'd probably not be able to move the next day. But at least it was Sunday.

She had gotten into her nightgown and robe and was about to go next door to tell Jason to come home when the phone rang. She stared at it for a moment before answering. No one ever called her. And if Jason wanted to stay up later, he would have come home and asked.

"Hello?" she said, her voice sounding tentative to her ears.

"Hi, Betts, how're you doing?"

No, don't let it be, she thought.

"Betts? Is that you?"

"Hello, Tom."

"How're things going in the big city?"

If he really cared, he wouldn't have taken so long to find out. "Jason's fine; everything's all right."

"Did you get a job yet, babe?"

"Yes." If she hadn't, they'd be starving by now.

"Pounding the old keyboard?"

She had forgotten his proclivity for clichés. "I'm working as a word processor for a law firm, Tom. They were willing to train me."

"Hey, that's great."

"Was there something you wanted?"

"As a matter of fact, there was. I'm thinking of taking Jase skiing over Christmas vacation and just wanted to firm it up with you."

"Oh, no—not for Christmas," she said without thinking. It wasn't that she'd be all alone as much as she was so looking forward to their first Christmas in New York.

"Well, look, Betts, I don't want to upset the apple-cart or anything. How about the week after Christmas? I thought I'd take him to Aspen."

There was no way she could deprive Jason of that. They all loved to ski, and she wouldn't be able to afford to take him. Plus she knew he missed his father.

"Well, that's okay with me, Tom. Why don't I get Jason and you can ask him yourself."

Without waiting for an answer she went down the

hall and knocked on the door to Abby's apartment.
Jason opened it.

"Your father's on the phone, honey."

"Dad," he yelled, then went racing for their apartment.

Abby lifted an inquiring brow.

"He wants to take him skiing over New Year's."

Abby nodded in understanding.

Betsy got back to the apartment just as Jason was
hanging up the phone.

"We're going skiing, Mom, just me and Dad. You
don't mind, do you?"

"Of course not, honey—not as long as we're together for Christmas."

"You know what I want for Christmas, Mom?"

"No, and I don't want to know. It's not even November yet, Jason."

"But you'll like it, Mom, and it won't even cost
you anything."

That would be a novelty. "All right, Jason, what
do you want for Christmas?"

"A kitten."

"I didn't know you liked cats."

"Well, you know, Dad was allergic to them,
so..."

"I'll think about it."

"Mom?"

"Yes?"

"Cats eat roaches."

Betsy smiled. "I certainly *will* think about it."

She spent most of Sunday heating her tired muscles
under an electric blanket and reading *The Times*,

which, she had discovered, was practically an all-day project. Jason was allowed to go down to his school playground with a friend to shoot some baskets in the afternoon, and to bring home food from McDonald's that night for their supper.

Betsy was usually sorry to see the weekend end, but she found she was perversely looking forward to her next encounter with the insidious Mr. Creme.

She was wrong when she said Abby could have been describing Tom. There was something about Nick that made him far sexier than she had ever found her husband to be. Not that their sex life hadn't been fine, but Tom had the kind of boyish good looks that might have appealed to her at nineteen but didn't do much for her at twenty-nine.

She remembered the way Nick had looked in his tight jeans, his leg muscles straining against the worn fabric, and the depth of his chest beneath his sweat shirt. She found the sheer bulk of him alone sexy, to say nothing of those brooding dark eyes or that strongly molded mouth. Tom had looked very much like her brothers; Nick had the kind of dark exotic looks she associated with men from the Mediterranean countries, and everyone knew how sexy *they* were.

Yes, there was an attraction there, and it was mutual. On her part it was a physical attraction; on his, perhaps physical too, but also a challenge to his ego. Oh, not that she didn't enjoy the verbal sparring; she'd be lying if she said she didn't. But that was just the outlet for the physical forces at play between them.

And was she going to do anything about it? No

way! She missed the steady sex life she had grown accustomed to in her marriage, missed the warmth of another body in her bed at night, but the answer to that wasn't having an affair. She wished she could enjoy casual sex the way the young women at the office seemed to, the way even Abby did at times, but she knew herself too well to think it would work for her. She had always romanticized sex, and nothing she told herself to the contrary could really alter those feelings.

She would have to feel very strongly about a man in order to have sex with him, and she knew that those strong feelings, combined with the sex, would surely result in her falling in love. And love was something she was very reluctant to risk experiencing again. She loved Jason, she loved Abby, and she was slowly falling in love with New York; loving a man at this point would be superfluous. To say nothing of disastrous if it involved an office Lothario the likes of Nicholas Creme. Men like him should be labeled WARNING: DANGEROUS TO YOUR HEALTH.

Like her, he was the survivor of a broken marriage, but unlike her, he was out to wreak his revenge on every woman who came into his orbit. He probably took sex about as seriously as eating a hamburger at McDonald's.

She would play verbal games with him in the office if that's what he wanted. Soon he would tire of them and move on to some new challenge, she was sure. As for her? Surviving in New York was enough of a challenge to her at the moment; she didn't need the challenge of a man, too.

Chapter Three

"If I had known you were in training, I wouldn't have invited you for a drink."

It was Monday night, all she had done was come directly to Nick's office to pick up her work, and now he was speaking in riddles. Maybe she should go out and come back in again.

Nick grinned. "You've got a good arm," he said, then added deprecatingly, "for a girl."

She could only stare at him, bewildered.

Nick leaned back in his chair, his hands clasped behind his neck. "I'm referring, of course, to your football prowess."

She could feel herself slowly turning red. "Oh. That," she mumbled. "Actually, I throw like a boy."

"Yes, I'll grant you that. Not like a *man*, of course, but like a boy."

She found herself glaring at him. "I really don't see the difference."

"Of course not. That's why you throw like a boy."

Calm yourself, she admonished. He's just trying to provoke you. "I *knew* I saw you in the crowd."

"I was sure you did."

"And you yelled at me; ruined my play." Just remembering it made her angry.

"A professional would have kept his mind on the game and not have been grandstanding." A supercilious smile crossed his face.

"Grandstanding?" The glare had turned to a look of fury. Why did this man always get to her like that? And why did she let him?

"Yes, grandstanding. Now, if you'd like some pointers—"

"I do not want any pointers!" She was practically yelling. In a business office. At one of the bosses. She closed her eyes and clenched her fists, willing herself to calm down.

She heard him chuckle. He seemed to actually enjoy making her lose her temper.

"How about a game of handball sometime?"

"What?"

"Not a date, just a friendly game between us 'boys.' "

"I don't play handball. I play tennis."

"Where I grew up we didn't have tennis courts."

"Where I grew up we didn't play handball," she countered frostily.

The look he gave her denoted his feelings that she had experienced a deprived childhood. Handball? What in the world was handball?

"Do you have any work for me?" she finally asked him.

He gave her a condescending look. "Do you think you've calmed down enough to do it?"

"I'm perfectly calm," she said through clenched teeth.

"You seem to have quite a temper, Ms. Miller."

"Not usually, Mr. Creme."

"Do I provoke you?"

"You certainly try to."

He grinned. "And I succeed, don't I?"

All too well, she thought. "I apologize for yelling at you, Mr. Creme. I'm ready to get to work now."

"But I'm not ready yet, Betsy. Why don't you take a seat? No, not on the couch, over here."

She took a seat in the proffered club chair next to his desk. *He probably thinks he's giving me a chance to admire his profile,* she thought to herself as he bent his head over the desk to write in some corrections. Instead, she stared past him out the window, where the lights were going on all over the city, turning New York into her idea of a Disneyland for adults.

When he finished and handed her the papers, Betsy got up to go.

"Do you mind if I ask you something, Betsy?"

"My minding or not has never stopped you before," she said sweetly.

"Are you a regular member of the team?"

She had to smile at that. "Actually, Saturday was something of a tryout for me."

"And did you make the team?"

She gave him a look of triumph. "They said I was their secret weapon."

"Of course, you do have some years and some weight on the rest of them," he said dampeningly.

Keep your skinny little actresses, she felt like hurling at him as she spun out of his office. If there was ever a more infuriating man, she certainly hadn't met him.

The document was very long, and she knew she had no chance of getting out early. At around ten, when she went to the kitchen for coffee, she ran into Christine.

"How's it going with Nick, Betsy?"

Betsy took down a large cup from the cupboard and filled it with strong black coffee. "I don't see how you could stand to work for him, Christine."

"Oh, Nick's easy to work for. Is he giving you a hard time?"

"I guess our personalities just clash." She couldn't help noticing Christine's tight sweater, plaid miniskirt, and white plastic boots.

Christine caught her glance and made a face. "Dreadful, isn't it? I had to come straight to work from an audition for a sixties teen-ager."

"Oh. Well, good luck on it."

"Thanks, but I won't get it. There must have been two thousand of us there in the same outfits, and some of them were real teen-agers."

That would be stiff competition, she had to admit. She wondered, not for the first time, how the actresses took so much rejection and still stayed committed to their ambitions.

"By the way, I hear you play football."

"Oh, no," Betsy said with dismay.

"I promise I won't tell anyone. I had brunch with Nicky on Sunday, and he mentioned seeing you in the park on Saturday. He asked me if I knew anything about it."

"I'm really embarrassed that he saw me." She

didn't add that what embarrassed her the most was his being a witness to her getting sacked.

"If you need exercise, you ought to join my dance class, Betsy. It's very good for the body and so much more feminine. Men don't really like jocks, you know."

Betsy held back her retort and told Christine that she would think about it. Jock indeed! She was beginning to think Nick and Christine deserved each other. She thought about Christine and Nick having brunch together. Brunch. Just the term sounded so New York. So sophisticated. All she ever had was breakfast, and that was usually Frosted Flakes with Jason.

It was after midnight when she finally finished, and only Lisa was still around finishing up a tape. She took the document to Nick, who thanked her politely, then got her coat and headed for the elevators. No sooner did the elevator arrive than Nick appeared and got in it beside her.

As they walked through the lobby together Betsy looked at her watch and said, "It's not very late."

Nick gave her a smile. "Is that a hint that you have time to go for a drink with me?"

She gave him a sideways glance of annoyance. "No, it's merely a hint that it's not too late for me to walk home."

He smiled, said good night, and got into his waiting cab, not even offering her a ride, which she had been sure would be forthcoming. Sometimes he was a Jekyll and Hyde.

She crossed Forty-second Street, heading south,

not noticing for the first block that a cab was following her until she had to stop at the light. When she did notice, she glared at its occupant, then ran across the street against the light and was halfway down the block before she heard the motor once again behind her. She couldn't believe he was being so childish as to follow her home in a taxi.

Three blocks from her building, the cab still on her trail, she let the taxi pull out in front of her at a light, then quickly backtracked a few yards and ducked into a neighborhood bar. She had only intended waiting there a minute, but the place was practically empty, and the bartender was eyeing her expectantly.

She sat down at one of the stools and ordered a beer. Seconds later a voice behind her said, "Can I buy you a drink, honey?"

Betsy ignored him as he took the stool beside her and ordered himself a beer. The bartender brought two, then hovered there as though Betsy might need some protection.

"I can't believe you followed me in a taxi," she finally said.

"Yeah, me neither. I've never done that before."

She chuckled. "What did you tell the driver, follow that pedestrian?"

He nodded. "He thought I was a nut."

"You *are* a nut."

"I'm having a drink with you, aren't I, and it's not even a date." His voice held a note of satisfaction.

"Not only don't I date, I also don't pick up men in bars."

He looked over at an empty booth. "Let's move over there where there's more privacy."

She glanced over and decided it looked innocuous enough, so she picked up her beer and followed him, settling herself on the other side of the booth.

He took out his pack of cigarettes and offered her one.

"No, thanks, I'm in training."

"Then you shouldn't be drinking beer."

"I doubt they serve Gatorade here."

"How come you're not drinking wine?"

"Why should I be drinking wine?"

"All the women I date drink wine. White wine."

"This isn't a date."

"I know, I know." He paused. "Isn't beer fattening?"

She glared at him, eyeing his bulk. "If it is, you shouldn't be drinking it, Mr. Creme."

"Listen, I didn't mean that personally. It's just that all the women I know are always on diets."

She was getting a little tired of hearing about all those women he knew.

"You look fine the way you are."

She ignored him.

"I mean it."

She took a long drink of her beer and felt herself start to relax. This wasn't such a bad idea having a drink after work; usually she was too keyed up by the time she got home from work to get to sleep. Maybe she'd start joining the others when they went out after work for drinks. She slid down in her seat a little and felt her knees touch his, but rather than quickly moving away, she stayed there, feeling too relaxed to care. Knees touching. Big deal!

"I hear you're divorced."

She sat up like a shot. "How could you 'hear.' I haven't told anyone."

He signaled to the bartender for two more beers, but she hardly noticed, so intent was she on his reply.

"I read your job application form."

Well, she really couldn't yell about that; he *was* one of the bosses. She remembered Abby telling her to be sure to put down that she was divorced, even though they weren't legally required to answer that question, but not to mention Jason. Abby assured her that being divorced sounded good, like she really needed a job, but that having a child didn't sound good, as mothers were out too often with sick children.

"I'm divorced, too," he was saying.

Now he was no doubt expecting sympathy. Two divorcés crying over their beer. If all else didn't work, that was always a good ploy, she imagined.

"My wife walked out on me."

Well, he wasn't going to get to her that way. "Probably with good reason," she told him caustically.

The bartender set two new beers in front of them, and Betsy saw with surprise that she had finished her first.

"*What* good reason," he growled.

She gave him a sweet smile. "Being taken with very young women doesn't just happen overnight," she told him pointedly. She expected him to get angry at her remark, defensive, but he looked amused instead.

"I can't help it—they're taken with me."

"And with a lot of encouragement, I'm sure."

"You jealous?"

"No, but your wife probably was."

"She had no reason to be."

He took a long swallow of beer, and Betsy did the same. It felt good being in a public place without a child for a change. She and Abby would have to come here sometime.

"What's the matter, your husband leave you for a younger woman?"

"No. As a matter of fact she was older."

He choked on his beer. *"Older?"*

"By several years."

He chuckled. "I like that. I think it shows class."

Betsy thought about it for a moment and found that she agreed with him. It *had* shown class on Tom's part. At least she hadn't been left for just a younger, firmer body. For the first time since the divorce she found she could smile about it.

"Didn't you try to get him back?"

She looked surprised. "No."

"Why the hell not?"

"I don't know. Pride, I guess, and anger. And I don't think I would have forgiven him for running around, anyway."

"No double standards for you, huh?"

"No."

"You took your marriage seriously?"

"Very seriously. And this really isn't any of your business."

"All you had to do was tell me to shut up."

"Consider yourself told."

He lighted a cigarette and loosened his tie. He looked tired, she thought, and no wonder. He was working days as well as most nights. She wondered when he had time to date all those women of his.

"I didn't run around. My wife left me to 'find herself.'"

Betsy couldn't help smiling at his morose tone. "And did she?"

"I don't know. The last thing I heard she was over in Greece, still looking. On my alimony."

"I refused alimony," she told him.

"What the hell for?"

She shrugged. "I wanted to be responsible for myself."

There was a momentary gleam in his dark eyes. "I should have married you."

"Why? So you could divorce me and not have to pay alimony?"

He grinned. "Well, when you put it like that. . ."

She drank down the rest of the second bottle of beer and felt so very relaxed that when he put his hand over hers on the table, she didn't even pull it away. She was just thinking that he wasn't so bad, that he just seemed to need someone to talk to, when he opened his big mouth again.

"Betsy, you really shouldn't take it so hard, you know. Not all men are like your husband. You'll find someone else."

She gave him an annoyed look and pulled her hand from beneath his. "Thanks, but I'm quite happy the way I am."

"You can't be happy without a man."

She looked at him and saw that he was serious. "I'll forget you said that, Nick." Her tone was threatening.

"Sorry, I never seem to say the right thing to you."

"You never *try*. Why did you read my application form?"

"I wanted to find out how old you were."

"I don't see why my age—"

"I'm tired of younger women."

Her eyes flashed. "I'm younger than you are."

"What's six years? Nothing." He waited for her agreement; none was forthcoming. "Why'd you marry him?"

She answered without thinking. "He played football better than I did. Why'd you marry your wife?"

"I was in love," Nick said, then added, "I play football better than you."

"I only have your word for that."

"Maybe we could go to the park someday and I could prove it."

"That would be a date."

He sunk his head in his hands and groaned. "Betsy, why don't you take a survey of all the women you know and see just how many of them would consider tossing a football around the park to be a date?"

As she thought about that she chuckled. "The only criteria is what *we* would think, Nick. Personally, it would be my idea of a terrific date."

"Then you agree?"

"No. I don't date."

A couple came into the bar thoroughly soaked, and Betsy and Nick looked toward the door.

"It's pouring," he groaned.

"I better get home," she said.

"I'll take you in a cab."

"I don't mind walking in the rain."

He gave her a look of disgust. "Don't be stupid—you'll get sick."

"I never get sick. I haven't even had a cold since I was a child."

"I'll walk you home." Now he had the air of a martyr about him.

"Nick—"

"Listen, it *is* late now, and anyway, you're feeling the beer. If you think I'm going to let some silly drunk—"

"I am *not* drunk."

He glared at her.

Betsy thought a moment. "Will you excuse me while I make a phone call?"

He nodded and ordered another beer.

Betsy went to the phone booth in the back and dialed Abby's number. A sleepy voice answered.

"It's me, Abby."

"You on your way home?"

"Yes. Listen, I'm in a bar with Nick—"

"He finally talked you into it, huh?"

"No. I'll explain it all later. Look, Abby, will you do me a favor?"

"Sure, kid."

"Would you take Jason and put him in his own

bed? I'll be home in a few minutes, but it's pouring out, and I'm sure Nick is going to want to come up for some coffee or something. I'd just like to have my little chaperon there when I arrive.''

"It sounds to me like you're setting him up.''

"Abby! Would I do a thing like that?''

"Hell, yes," muttered Abby. "Consider it done, and I can't wait to hear the latest.''

Nick looked up when she came back to the booth. "Did you call us a cab?''

"It's only three blocks.''

They stood in the doorway, putting on their coats and looking out at the rain.

"We might as well go," said Nick. "It doesn't look as though it's going to let up.''

"Nick, why don't you get yourself a cab? There's no point in us both getting wet.''

"I'm walking you home.''

What a stubborn man! "Look outside, Nick. No muggers are going to be out in that weather.''

"You never know," he said, grabbing her arm and pulling her out in the rain.

The rain did two things for Betsy very quickly: It sobered her up and soaked her to the skin. It wasn't the softly falling rain she had envisaged; this rain was hard and relentless, and a cold wind whipped it around their ducked heads as they hurried in the direction of her building. And every time they passed someone else out in the foul weather, Nick leaned down to her and muttered, "Potential mugger." By the time they got to her building they both looked like drowned animals and there wasn't a taxi in sight.

"Look, could I call a cab from your apartment?"

She gave him a sweet smile. "Sure, I'll even fix you a cup of coffee."

She didn't blame him for looking suspicious at that remark, but then he probably figured it was the beer talking.

She opened the door to the apartment quietly, turned on one of the lamps, then went to the kitchen to put the kettle on.

"It's instant," she warned him.

"I'm used to it."

He was standing there in a puddle, and she took his coat and hung it in the shower, then did the same with hers. "Sit down, Nick."

"I'll get everything wet."

"It doesn't matter."

She was glad when he finally sat down on the couch. Standing up, he made the apartment seem twice as small as usual. He was looking through the morning paper when she brought in the coffee. "Do you mind if I change into something dry?"

He practically smirked. "Not at all. By all means change into something more comfortable."

She was trying not to laugh in the bathroom as she changed into the jeans and sweat shirt she kept on the hook behind the door, then she toweled some of the water out of her hair. The fool was probably picturing her coming back out in a black lace negligee.

His face fell at her appearance. As he was taking up most of the small couch, she settled herself on the floor on the other side of the coffee table. He was looking cold and wet and bedraggled, and she had a sudden urge to wrap him up in warm blankets and hug him. *Just my motherly instinct,* she mused, but pitiful as he looked, he was still sexy as hell.

"You've got a nice place," he said at last.

"It's awfully small..."

"But cozy. Where's the bed?"

She got to her knees. "In the bedroom. Would you like to see?"

His look of surprise turned to one of reproval. "Don't be in such a rush, Betsy; we hardly know each other."

She started to laugh at what he was thinking. The man must think she was drunk and taking leave of her senses. It struck her funnier and funnier by the moment until she was almost rolling on the floor in laughter, quite unable to control herself.

"Are you okay, Mom?"

The small voice penetrated her laughter, and she got to her knees to see Jason standing in the doorway to the bedroom, rubbing his eyes and looking at her woefully.

"Your mother just has a weird sense of humor, kid," Nick said dryly.

Jason was nodding in agreement. "Yeah, I know. Who're you?"

"You can call me Nick."

Jason's eyes widened. "Oh, it's you. All I ever hear around here from Mom and Abby is Nick, Nick, Nick."

"Go to bed, Jason," said Betsy.

"Oh, really?" said Nick, sounding interested.

"Jason! Go to bed this instant."

"Just what have you been hearing about me?" Nick was smiling fondly at Jason.

"I don't know—I never pay any attention."

"Jason, if you're not in bed in ten seconds..."

"Are *you* going to bed now, Mom?"

Nick was shaking with laughter.

"Not quite yet, Jason."

With a grin at Nick, Jason turned and went back into the bedroom, this time closing the door between the two rooms.

Nick gave her a wicked look. "This has got to be the greatest hustle known to living man. A classic! You lure me up to your apartment, you change out of your wet things, you ask me if I want to see your bed, and all the time, lurking in the next room, is your secret weapon. Beautiful!"

"I did *not* lure you up here," she mildly protested.

"Don't worry about it. I knew you had a kid."

"You couldn't have known that."

"Listen, you may be a nut, but even you wouldn't hang around Central Park by yourself, trying to get into a football game. There had to be a kid involved."

She had to admit that sounded logical. "Would you like some more coffee?"

"Sure." He held out his cup to her. "And I'd also like to hear what you and Abby have been saying about me. I assume that's Abby from the office?"

"Yes. We baby-sit for each other."

"And I'm the prime target of conversation?"

"Don't get carried away," she told him. "Jason probably heard your name *once*." She could see he didn't believe her for a minute.

She brought in the coffee and pointed out the phone to him. "Hadn't you better call your cab?"

"Trying to get rid of me?"

"I thought I was at least doing it politely."

"Oh, you were. How about going to the theater with me Saturday night?"

She gave him a wary look. "No, Nick."

"You like opera, ballet?"

She did, but that was beside the point. "No, thank you, Nick."

He grinned. "How about a hockey game at the Garden?"

Her eyes widened, making her look very much like Jason at that moment. "An ice hockey game?"

"I figured that would get to you."

She gave him a tentative smile. "Thanks, but no."

"And bring the kid, of course."

Her eyes narrowed. "Is that blackmail?"

"Just a little coercion."

"No, but thank you for the idea. Jason would love a hockey game, and I haven't been to one in years."

"It's the Black Hawks and the Rangers."

Her eyes widened again. "Really?"

His expression softened. "No, I just threw that in as an added inducement. I don't know who the Rangers are playing. Look, Betsy, it won't be a date—hell, you can even pay for your own tickets. We'll meet at the door, sit together, and then when it's over I'll even let you walk home alone. It's not far from here, anyway."

"I've never been to Madison Square Garden."

"It's great. You'll love it."

Her mind was a jumble of thoughts, and she could feel herself wavering. Jason would be so excited, and it would be good for him to have the companionship of a man for a change. And she loved hockey. She wondered how Nick could possibly be free on a Saturday night, or why he'd prefer their company to one of his usual friends.

She nodded. "All right. As long as it's not a real date." She expected to see a look of triumph in his eyes, but he just looked pleased.

"Don't worry about it. I don't take my dates to hockey games."

Then, as though he wanted to leave before she changed her mind, he picked up the phone and called for a taxi. Despite the rain there was one in the neighborhood, and he got up to leave.

Betsy got his coat from the bathroom and held it while he slipped his arms in. When he turned around, they were very close together, so close, she could smell the wet wool and a hint of some after-shave. He put his hand under her chin and lifted her face. She caught her breath, suddenly wondering what it would feel like to be kissed by those firm lips, feel the dark roughness of his face against her own smooth one, run her fingers through his shaggy wet hair. She lowered her eyes, afraid her thoughts might be revealed there.

"Don't worry, I'm not going to try anything," he said in his gruff voice. "I don't want to do anything to scare you off at this point."

He opened the door easily and stepped out into the hall. "Are you sure you have enough locks on this door?"

Betsy looked at the three existing ones, two of which she never bothered to use. "I would say so."

"You can never be sure. Maybe you should get one of those police locks."

"Nick..." she warned him.

"I wasn't worried about you, I was thinking of the kid."

"Good night, Nick," she said pointedly.

He grinned. "Good night, Betsy."

She closed the door, locked one lock, and stood for a moment shaking her head. Things were not going as she had planned. No matter what had been said, Saturday night certainly sounded like a date to her. Of course, Jason would be along, so Nick wouldn't be able to get too personal. But if she went out with him once, wouldn't he presume she'd say yes again?

She went into the bathroom and looked in the mirror. Her damp hair was curling up around her head, her eyes were bright, her cheeks were flushed. She thought her face had an expectant look. Had she really wanted to kiss him? Him in particular? Or was she feeling the absence of a man in general? She had always had an affectionate nature—was that all it was? No, if she was going to be honest with herself, she'd have to admit it was Nick she had felt like kissing. There was something very sensuous about the man; something that made her aware of him every moment he was around.

She was going to have to tread very carefully around that man, or all her good intentions were going to go right down the drain and she would find herself added to his list of available women, a thought that didn't please her at all.

She took her wet clothes that were in a pile on the floor and hung them up on the shower rod, then ran the water in the tub for a hot bath. The rain was coming down strong, hitting with fierce intensity against the skylight in the ceiling. She shivered as she stepped into the warm water. The heat was off for the night, and she felt chilled right through.

The thought of Nick warming her bed, warming her body, flashed across her mind, and she felt momentarily shaken. Was that what she wanted? An affair with Nick Creme? No. Part of her might want it, the part that felt bereft after the closeness of ten years of marriage. To be blunt, her body might be lusting after Mr. Creme, but her mind wanted no part of it. He used women to bolster his male ego, and to him she was merely a challenge—one woman who was refusing to succumb to his considerable charm.

Oh, well, she'd get some good advice from Abby, she was sure. Abby would straighten her out. She hoped.

Chapter Four

"Of course you're attracted to Nick; practically every woman in the office is, so why should you be immune? All you've got to do is keep the whole thing in its proper perspective."

Abby was serving croissants that morning, and Betsy was doefully eyeing her third. "What do you mean?"

Abby lit a cigarette, then waved the smoke away from her face. "I mean that being attracted to a man doesn't mean you've got to end up married to him. Look at Nick. He's sure attracted to women, but you don't see him rushing out to tie the knot again. You're sensible, Betsy; you can handle it."

If I'm not sensible enough to stop at two croissants, Betsy thought ruefully, taking one, *then I really don't know.* She looked across the table at Abby, as usual admiring the way her friend looked. She was medium height and slimly built, and had a liking for bits and pieces of clothes rather than dresses or matched outfits. There was a flair to the clothes that she wore, the kind of flair Betsy always associated with Parisiennes, although she had never actually seen a Parisienne. Betsy had shopped with her in enough thrift shops to know where she picked up those bits and pieces, but she had to admit to never seeing their potential until Abby turned them into high fashion.

"You might think I'm sensible, Abby, but there's something you don't know about me." She was eyeing her fourth croissant and looked up to see Abby looking at her in amusement.

"And what is it I don't know about you?"

"I'm a romantic."

Abby laughed. "I knew that two minutes after I met you. I think it was when you said living in New York was like being in a movie."

Betsy still felt that way but decided not to say so.

Carla made her entrance from the bathroom with her hair in numerous messy braids, each one tied with a different color of yarn at the end. Betsy took one look and burst out laughing, earning her a venomous look from the child.

"You've got to be kidding," Abby said dryly.

Carla's lower lip pushed out. "A lot of girls in my class wear their hair this exact same way."

"A lot of girls in your class are black," countered Abby.

"You mean I have to be black to wear my hair like this?"

"Either that or have a very patient mother who feels like braiding five hundred braids every morning. I'm not a very patient mother, Carla."

Carla was still standing her ground.

"*Carla!*"

"Oh, all right, but you're always trying to stifle my creative instincts." The bathroom door slammed after her.

"I can't believe her vocabulary," Betsy gasped.

"All due to television, I'm afraid. What are you going to do today, Betts?"

"I thought I'd go to the UN."

"Again?"

"I wish you'd go with me sometime, Abby; you just don't know how interesting it is."

"When I was in school we were always being dragged there, and that's exactly what I thought it was—a drag!"

"Maybe you'd like it better now."

Abby poured them each another cup of coffee. "Why don't you try to get a job there if you like it so much?"

"As what, a guide? Even they speak more than one language. I'm not qualified to work there."

"So go to school and learn another language."

"But it would take me years to get fluent."

Abby gave her a serious look. "But don't you see? We've *got* years. And most of them ought to be spent doing something we really enjoy. I think having been married makes us tend to think our lives are over, when actually you could say they've just begun."

"What about you, Abby? Do you like what you're doing?"

Abby got up and started clearing off the table. "Right now it suits me. I like the money and I like our arrangement. But I've been talking to the paralegals at work, and they've almost got me convinced to take the course and be one myself. It's for only a few months, and when I finished they'd give me a job there and I'd be making a lot more. To say nothing of having my own office. Why don't you think about it, too?''

Betsy had thought about it when she first started working for the company, but she found what she did more interesting than the work of the paralegals. They spent most of their time doing legal research for the attorneys, and Betsy didn't fancy sitting in the law library all day.

Jason came in. His shoes said Nike, his pants said Levi's, his shirt had a picture of Snoopy on it, and the jacket he was carrying had his Glenview little league team name on the back. Jason was a firm advocate of advertising.

"Did you hear where you're going Saturday night?" Abby asked him.

Jason looked at his mother. "Not Indian food again, I hope."

"We're going to a hockey game at the Garden. With Nick." She watched closely for his reaction. Jason had never seen her with any man but his father, and she wasn't sure how he'd take it.

"A *hockey* game! Fantastic!"

"With Nick," she repeated.

"Great. Are you coming along too, Mom?"

Betsy looked a little put out, which made Abby laugh.

"Yeah, your mom's going along to chaperon you," she joked.

"What a great Saturday. A football game *and* a hockey game. Wow."

Carla made an encore with only one braid down her back, which Abby redid for her before the four of them set out.

All day long Betsy couldn't stop thinking about what Abby had said. The morning session in the Security Council wasn't that exciting, so she turned the dial to Russian so as not to be distracted from her thoughts. She began to think about her life. She had been a freshman in college when she had met Tom, had married him the summer before her sophomore year, and midway through that year had gotten pregnant and dropped out of school. All of which gave her only a year and a half of college credits. Now that she was no longer married she had thought of going back, of course, but she'd only be able to take a couple of courses at a time and the thought of years before she got a degree—and probably a useless degree at that as far as the job market went—had always discouraged her. But Abby was right. Even if it took her ten years to prepare herself for a career, she'd have many years after that in which to practice that career, and the time to begin was now.

What she'd really love to do would be something concerned with foreign affairs. She was really developing a passion for it. She read *The New York Times* from cover to cover every day, but the parts on world affairs were what really interested her. And she truly did find sitting in on the UN fascinating, even when they weren't concerned with a crisis. Being an interpreter there might be interesting, but there were so many native New Yorkers who spoke two languages fluently already, she would certainly not be in demand. And they weren't really *doing* anything; they were simply interpreting what was being done.

How she longed to be someone who really did something, like the people below her now, making

speeches and arguing and voting on things that actually helped shape the world. She was aware that
some of them were political appointees, but others
must be professionals. A profession that she might
possibly be able to learn.

She started to get excited just thinking about her
future. She decided that the next morning, instead of
going to the UN, she would go down to New York
University and get a copy of their course catalog, and
maybe, if possible, talk to an adviser there. They
must have a program in something that would suit
her interests; maybe political science for a start.

There was a motion on the floor to censure Israel,
and now the Israeli delegate was going to speak.
Betsy found him quite eloquent with his British accent, and she took off her headset to listen.

THE SEMESTER was already in progress at NYU, so
things weren't too hectic, and the registration office
not only gave Betsy their catalog, but sent her along
to see Dr. Manzer, the head of the Political Science
Department.

Betsy knocked at his office door, then went inside.
The room was like the man himself: small, purpose-
ful, and scrupulously neat. There were two upright
chairs, a bare desk except for a black telephone, and
only one object decorating the walls—a framed map
of the world. There were no books, no papers, not
even a file cabinet, as though the man held all knowledge in his head and considered it a weakness in
others that they couldn't do the same.

Betsy took the chair he offered and, at his urging,

began to tell him hesitantly about her half-formulated ideas of what she'd like to do.

"You have an interest in foreign affairs."

It was a statement, not a question, but Betsy found herself nodding in agreement.

"An *avid* interest."

"Yes, sir." Something in him seemed to compel that form of address.

"Well, I'll tell you what I tell all the others who come in here, but none of them listen to me. They all picture themselves as eventual ambassadors in some European capital; not a realistic one among them."

Betsy, who had been envisioning herself in the same way, stayed silent.

"The Middle East—that's where it's all happening, pardon the slang. Learn Arabic, young lady. Hardly anyone does, and one of these days that's going to be a disadvantage."

"Yes, sir; I can see that by reading the papers."

"You read the papers? Good, good. Not many students do, you know. Oh, maybe *The Village Voice*, to see what rock group is currently in town."

Betsy, who enjoyed reading *The Voice*, made no comment.

"Well? You still want my advice?"

"Yes, please."

"Get in the Political Science Department, take a minor in Arabic—get fluent in it—then, when you're finished with your degree, go up to Columbia and get a master in Middle-Eastern Studies. You'll be way ahead of the crowd. Way ahead. Of course, those

Arabs don't like dealing with women, but that's just too bad, isn't it?''

The Arabs not liking to deal with women was practically the deciding factor. Like some other people she could think of, Betsy also liked a challenge. She also very much liked the intelligent man seated across from her.

"Thank you, Dr. Manzer; I think I'll do just that."

He looked surprised. "You mean you're going to take my advice?"

"I think it's excellent advice."

He gave her a pleased look. "Well, now, you say you completed a year and a half of college at Northwestern?"

"Yes."

"Excellent school. That means you probably got a lot of the basics out of the way. I'll give you a little more advice, young lady. You appear to be serious, and it's too late for you to get into any of the classes this semester, so what I suggest you do..."

He opened a drawer and removed a pad of paper and a freshly sharpened pencil, writing something down on the pad and then handing it to her.

"I suggest you pick up this basic book on Arabic at the bookstore and start studying on your own. That way you'll have a head start in January and you won't lose your enthusiasm in the meantime."

She got up to leave, and he stood to shake her hand. "It was a pleasure, Ms. Miller; I don't often get to talk to students as serious as you. You're a little older than the rest, aren't you?"

"I'm twenty-nine."

"Excellent, excellent. You'll find that an advantage, I think. This time around you won't be concerned with meeting boys and Saturday night dates. You'll just be interested in getting an education, so that's exactly what you'll get. Thank you for coming in and seeing me, and I look forward to seeing you again next semester."

Betsy left the Political Science building and walked a couple of blocks south to Le Figaro, a coffee shop in the heart of Greenwich Village that she had been to once before with Abby. Both of them loved the Village and would have liked to live there, but the rents were very high if you could even find an apartment.

Le Figaro had been a famous meeting place for writers and Bohemians in the twenties; now it was mostly a student hangout. One of the local artists was being exhibited on the walls, and even though it was a weekday a guitarist was sitting in one corner, singing and playing folk songs.

She ordered an asparagus omelette, knowing she was definitely going to have their chocolate mousse pie for dessert, and decided it would be almost as much fun to go to school in the Village as it would be to live there. Being in the area frequently, she would be able to browse in the bookshops and shop in the small specialty stores. And if she had classes on a day when Jason and Carla were off from school, she could bring them down to Washington Square Park to roller-skate.

She ate her omelette, her thoughts on school, but when the chocolate mousse pie was placed in front of her, she gave it her undivided attention. She was a pretty good cook herself, but never had she concocted anything this delicious.

When she was finished she walked over to Barnes & Noble Bookstore on Fifth Avenue and Eighteenth Street, from where the local schools got their textbooks. She found it was two buildings on either side of the street, and went first into The Annex, which carried the textbooks. She got a large tome on beginning Arabic, then crossed the street to look in the other store, since she still had some time.

It turned out to be a reader's paradise. There were more books for sale than she had ever seen in one place, and table after table had books on sale for only one or two dollars. She found a book for Abby on learning to be a paralegal, one for Jason on ice hockey, and even a book on gypsies for Carla. She was feeling so pleased with herself she walked all the way home, not even minding her heavy load.

Her first shock was when she opened her textbook and saw what Arabic looked like. She took a pen and piece of paper, made some squiggles and dots, then compared it to the book. It looked exactly like Arabic, only she had done hers from left to right and they did it exactly opposite. It looked like no language she had ever seen. She was about to give it up there and then, but she reminded herself that little Arab children could learn it. And if children could learn it, she'd be darned if she couldn't.

Betsy, Jason, and Carla were all reading their books when Abby got home from work.

"My mom's going to be an Arab," Jason told her.

Abby didn't even look fazed. "Carla wants to be a gypsy, you want to be an Arab; isn't anyone satisfied with what they are?"

Betsy told Abby all about Dr. Manzer as she got ready for work. "And it was all due to you, Abby. You're right—I've got my whole life ahead of me and I want to spend it doing something that really interests me."

"That's great, and you can take classes while the kids are in school."

Betsy nodded happily.

"Incidentally, Nick's out of town for the rest of the week, so it's just as well you have something else to occupy your mind."

"Where'd he go?" she asked, finding that the thought of work without him around didn't please her.

"Washington. On business."

"Nick, Nick, Nick," muttered Jason, earning him a swat on the rear end from Betsy.

NICK RETURNED ON FRIDAY, but Betsy only saw him briefly as she arrived for work and he was leaving.

"I'll let you know tomorrow where and what time we'll meet for the game," he told her.

"I'm not working tomorrow," she reminded him.

He grinned. "I thought I'd catch your game."

"My *football* game?"

"Yeah."

The last thing she wanted was Nick out there watching her act like a ten-year-old. A very large ten-year-old, at that. "Don't you have anything better to do on Saturdays?'' she asked rather testily.

But he merely said no, then left before she could argue with him any further.

ALTHOUGH IT HAD RAINED ALL NIGHT, the sun came out on Saturday, and an eager Jason was dressed and ready to go when Betsy woke up. He even had a cold bowl of cereal ready for her. When she told him she preferred coffee first, he looked so disappointed that she sat right down and ate the cereal, then made herself coffee. She dressed the same as the previous week, but added some red leg warmers to protect her knees, just in case she should happen to be tackled to the ground again.

Nick was already there when they arrived at the playing field. In gray sweat pants and sweat shirt, he looked very masculine and halfway professional as he stood throwing passes to the boys. Betsy watched him for a moment, trying to figure out if he was better than she was and whether her spot on the team had already been usurped.

Nick saw her and walked over. At least he had the grace to look a bit sheepish, she noted.

''Just warming up the guys,'' he muttered.

''I thought maybe you were trying to take my spot,'' she snapped.

''Hey, Nick,'' said Jason, noticing him for the first time.

''What do you say, Jason?''

''Why are you wearing that outfit if you just came to watch?'' Betsy wanted to know.

''I've decided to coach the team.''

"*You* decided? Doesn't the team have anything to say about it?"

He grinned. "They seem delighted. You're going to start having regularly scheduled games against other teams soon, you know."

Betsy turned away from him to greet the other members of the team and found that Nick had already set it up so that they'd practice for a half hour and then go into a game.

The first twenty minutes of practice were bad enough. Nick had taken it upon himself to come up with some new plays that they all practiced, even though Betsy had thought that that was the quarterback's prerogative and had thought up a few herself during the week. They clashed. She gave in not very gracefully, but had to admit to herself his were brilliantly conceived plays. Then, with a sidelong glance at Betsy, Nick announced that they were going to practice getting through the quarterback's protection. Meaning Betsy was going to be the target!

The play was called, Betsy dropped back with the ball, and then watched with horror as a herd of white rhino crashed through the players giving her protection, and she was able to identify it as Nick. Lunging for her body, he propelled her to the ground, which was sodden and muddy from a week of intermittent rain. She could feel her body sinking into the squishy mud as, at the same time, she felt Nick's body crushing her from above.

The breath was knocked out of her by more than the tackle. She could feel the pressure of his hard body against the length of hers, and it was having an effect on her that had nothing to do with football. She had never before thought the game at all erotic, but now, lying in the soft bed of mud, pinned down by Nick's weight, she began to reassess her thinking. She had an almost overwhelming urge to wrap her arms around his body and pull him even closer to her. She looked up into dark, knowing eyes only a space away from her own.

"Yes, it would be nice, wouldn't it," he drawled, "but we seem to have an audience."

Betsy glanced over to see the ring of boys circling them and came to her senses, trying to shove Nick off her. He got to his feet, put out a hand to help her up, and realized the back side of her was covered with mud. She was certainly not going to be in any shape to walk home down Fifth Avenue.

The game went well despite the fact that the quarterback was distracted every second by Nick's presence on the sidelines. He would call her over to give her a play, pat her on the rear end as she ran back onto the field, and leave her with this great desire to do well in order to earn the pat on the back she knew would be forthcoming. She was clearly becoming besotted with him but was having too much fun to worry about it.

The game broke up at four, and Nick walked Betsy and Jason out of the park. He was between them, holding each of their hands, and Betsy, in a noticeably euphoric state, didn't even protest. She found that she was beginning to really care about Nick, but instead of it distressing her, she found it felt good.

"You know, that's another thing I like about you," Nick said out of nowhere.

She felt the squeezing of her hand and looked up at him. "What's that?"

"In addition to not being a flirt, you also don't give a damn about how you look. Of course, I hope I don't happen to see one of our clients when I'm in such disreputable company."

Betsy tried to pull her hand away, but he held on firmly.

"Mom's learning to be an Arab," voiced Jason for no reason at all.

Nick looked down at her. "Really? What brought this on?"

She found herself telling Nick all about the UN and going down to NYU. He seemed genuinely interested and asked lots of questions about what kind of work she'd eventually like to do. He also told her a little about his years in Washington with the Internal Revenue Service and how much he had enjoyed the work.

"Then why did you leave?" she asked.

He shrugged. "I got to the top of the pay scale, and my wife decided we needed more money to live on. It's nice down there, though; I miss it. That's where you ought to go for your graduate work, you know."

"That's a long way off at the moment."

"You know, it's funny—my wife's trying to find herself, and you're really doing it."

She smiled up at him. "I am, aren't I. Now all I have to do is learn to decipher Arabic."

"Have you given any thought to any of the federal agencies? The Treasury Department, the FBI, the

CIA? You're the adventurous type. I'm surprised you don't want to be a spy.''

"Oh, spying wouldn't suit me.''

"Why not?''

"I usually say the first thing that comes into my head. I'm sure that spies with big mouths don't last long.''

He laughed. "Yes, I've noticed that trait.'' He let go of her hand and put his arm around her shoulders.

They reached Fifty-ninth Street, where Nick hailed a taxi, then left it standing while he arranged to meet them at the ticket booth at seven thirty. "I'd offer you a ride, but I know your proclivity for walking.''

"I want to ride with Nick,'' said Jason.

Betsy told him that athletes had to stay in shape by walking, and the two of them said good-bye to Nick and headed home.

Betsy found herself spending an inordinate amount of time in the bathroom, preparing for that evening. Nick might think she didn't care about how she looked, but that wasn't true. She soaked the mud off herself in the shower and found she had to wash her hair twice to get it clean. She made up her face, using mascara, blush, and lip gloss, then put Jason into the tub while she got dressed.

She realized she had more clothes and jewelry than the people she worked with, but seldom wore more than just the things she had purchased for work in case it looked like she was living beyond her salary. Not that she was; they were just residue from her marriage and didn't mean much to her. But tonight she found herself digging out a black cashmere sweater with a V neck and a nice pair of plaid wool slacks. She fastened a gold chain with a gold coin hanging from it around her neck and put on the slim gold watch she hardly ever wore anymore. She got into short black leather boots, then took a red wool cape out of the closet to wear. She had originally intended to wear just jeans and a sweat shirt, but she decided she wanted to look nice for Nick. After all, he was used to taking out some pretty chic women.

When Jason was ready to go in an assortment of clean, well-advertised clothes, they set off for the Garden. It was only a few blocks away, and they arrived early, which was just as well, as there was a long line of people waiting to buy tickets. When she got to the head of the line she purchased three tickets, then turned to see Nick coming up to them.

"If you buy my ticket, it's a date," he told her seriously.

She immediately told him the price and insisted he reimburse her on the spot, much to his enjoyment.

He was dressed in black wool slacks, a camel-colored turtleneck sweater, and a leather jacket, and their eyes seemed to admire each other for a moment before they went in to take their seats.

Nick sat between them, and Jason besieged him with questions up until the game started, and then they were all too immersed in the spectacle to talk at all, only cheering and screaming at the action going on in front of them. Betsy liked the way Nick acted with Jason; he wasn't condescending like some people are with children, but treated him more like a friend, and Jason reciprocated.

While part of Betsy was concentrated on the game, another part was aware every moment of Nick's large presence beside her. Their shoulders and arms were pressed together, their legs touched often, and once he even reached out and grabbed her knee in excitement. At one point a spectacular goal was scored and, when the three of them jumped up to cheer, Nick hugged them both to him for a moment, and Betsy felt herself wanting to hug him back. It was a traitorous thought, but she almost wished Jason weren't along and it were a real date.

She felt like going someplace quiet and dim with him afterward, maybe with candles on the tables and soft music. A place where they could be alone and really talk, get to know each other. Maybe even dance. She was thinking about their dancing together, their bodies pressed close together, his lips moving softly against her hair, when he pulled her out of her seat and she realized she had completely missed a goal being scored. She gave her head a rueful shake, trying to drive out the image of Nick and get back to the game, but it wouldn't work. He was definitely taking precedence over the game!

She wondered if she had been lonely and hadn't known it. After all, he was the first man who had paid any attention to her since her divorce, and now suddenly she seemed to be going overboard with her reactions. But in order to be lonely you have to be lonely for someone, and that hadn't been the case. She guessed it was just that being out with a man made her feel young again, and it had been a good many years since she had been with any man but her husband. She'd better watch it or Dr. Manzer would be proved wrong, and she *would* be looking forward to Saturday night dates instead of getting an education. And she didn't want that to happen. No, she certainly didn't. . . .

When the intermission came Nick got up and took orders for food. He lifted a brow when Betsy said three hot dogs and two beers, but didn't say anything.

"Nick's neat. I'm glad he's our friend, Mom," said Jason, clearly excited about being out at a live hockey game.

After the game Nick just happened to mention to Jason that he thought he'd walk around and try to find a place to get some ice cream before he went home, which was rather devious of him in Betsy's opinion.

"Nick, there's a great ice-cream place a block away from where we live," Jason informed him eagerly, clearly thinking ice cream was a good idea.

Nick raised a brow in Betsy's direction.

She hesitated a moment, not wanting him to know how reluctant she was to end the evening with him, then nodded. "Come along. They do have good ice cream."

Nick had a hot fudge sundae and watched with growing admiration as Betsy and Jason each consumed a gigantic banana split, then Jason once more took the initiative and asked Nick if he wanted to see the book on hockey his mom had bought him.

Nick professed a great interest in seeing the book, then grinned at Betsy and said he guessed he was stuck with walking them home.

When Nick sneezed for the third time on the way to the apartment, Jason asked him why he kept sneezing. "You were doing it at the game, too," he said in an accusing voice.

"Because some nut made me walk her home in the rain, and I got a cold as a result."

Betsy looked at him with concern. "I didn't know you had a cold."

"That's because you haven't seen me all week. I thought I had it licked, but I guess not."

She felt a little guilty but told herself that he was a grown man and should have known better than to sit in the cold and watch a hockey game and then eat ice cream if he was sick. And she hadn't made him walk her home!

It had been a long, tiring day for Jason, and he had only gotten to page two of the book he was showing Nick before he started falling asleep. He didn't even protest when Betsy suggested he go to bed, but was half undressed before he got to the bedroom, and when she went in a few minutes later he had fallen asleep on top of the covers. She lifted him up, pulled the blankets over him, then went back to the living room, closing the bedroom door behind her.

She supposed Nick would leave now, but she really didn't want him to. She wasn't tired at all and she found she preferred his company to curling up in bed with a book. She wasn't going to ask him to stay, though. But knowing him, he'd probably think of a reason. She looked at him sitting there, overpowering her small couch, looking incredibly sexy in that turtleneck sweater that strained across his chest muscles. If it was up to her, he'd dress like that all the time. Forget about suits; they made him look far too businesslike. Oh, dear, now she was beginning to think like a wife. Or maybe it was that she was so used to supervising Jason's dressing.

He was looking at her through lazy, half-closed eyes. They were on her face, then moved down to where the vee of her sweater met between the fullness of her breasts. They lingered there a moment, warming her in some inexplicable way, then he made a halfhearted attempt to get up off the couch.

"I guess it's time for me to go," he said, sounding as though he wanted to be persuaded otherwise.

She could at least act like a good hostess, she thought, moving into the room. After all, she'd offer any friend a cup of coffee before they left. "Would you like some coffee, Nick?"

He settled back on the couch. "I'd rather have something stronger."

"How about some brandy?"

He smiled at her. "Sounds good."

She thought of the beer and the hot dogs and the banana split and hoped that the brandy wouldn't clash with them in some way. She brought the bottle and two snifters into the living room and set them down on the coffee table, then put a record of French ballads on the stereo, turned down low. She had no idea what the songs were about, but anything in French sounded vastly romantic to her. With just the one lamp lit it was almost the scenario she had envisioned at the Garden.

She sat down next to him on the couch and poured

them each some brandy, then handed him his glass. She thought perhaps he'd say something like, "To us," but he merely gave her an amused look.

"Soft music, brandy, the kid in bed—what is this, Betsy, a seduction scene?"

Betsy gave him a sidelong glance. "Maybe." She took a long drink of the brandy and felt its immediate warmth enveloping her.

He chuckled. "Don't kid me—this isn't even a date."

"Dates are for high school kids," she said, wondering what his reaction would be.

He laughed. "That's where you're wrong. In high school I was always so nervous on dates, I never enjoyed them."

Betsy thought about that and conceded he might have a point. As she recalled, dating had always been rather traumatic. She'd worry about what she would wear and how she would look, worry about whether the boy would like her or not. Then, if he did like her, she'd worry about whether he was going to try anything, and if he did, what she should do. To say nothing of the major trauma if you didn't have a date for Saturday night and suffered the indignity of having to stay home with your parents and watch TV.

In a way it had been a relief to get married and leave all that behind her. But she supposed it would be different now. She was much more self-confident about herself, and sex was no longer a big mystery, half scary and half exciting. And yet at this time, in this city, casual sex seemed to be part and parcel of the dating game, and to her it just wasn't that casual.

On the other hand, she *was* thinking of sex with Nick. Did that mean she was in favor of casual sex, or was it that she sensed with Nick it wouldn't be casual?

He was eyeing her speculatively. "What's the matter with you tonight, Betsy? You haven't put me down once."

"Does that bother you?"

"Not a hell of a lot."

Why doesn't he just turn around and kiss me? she was thinking to herself, concentrating in her mind on him doing just that, as though through some sort of mental telepathy he would get her message and act upon it. But she obviously wasn't getting through, because now he was lighting a cigarette and looking over at her shelf of books. She supposed in this liberated society she could make the first move, but she knew she wouldn't. She might be learning to be more assertive in many ways, but so far that wasn't one of them. Anyway, he had been the pursuer in this relationship so far; why was he now acting so diffident? She sighed, and he turned to look at her.

"Have you ever thought of getting married again?"

That was about the last thing she had expected him to say, and she was too surprised at first to answer. "Several times," she finally said, then saw his look of surprise and amended it. "In theory only, you understand." Of course she had thought about it; she had spent hours discussing the subject with Abby.

"What conclusion did you reach?"

"That it wouldn't work for me. I'm learning to be independent, self-sufficient, and I like that."

"And that's not possible when you're married to someone?"

She turned to him, wanting him to understand. "Not if you love that person. Love makes you pervert your own independence and self-sufficiency. After a while you find yourself living for the other person and not yourself. At least you do if you're a woman."

"It needn't be like that."

"Maybe not, but it usually is."

"Yeah. It usually is." He reached for a cigarette, then seemed to change his mind and put the pack back into his pocket. "I guess I better be going."

She didn't say anything, just sat looking at him, her eyes wide and questioning.

"Don't you want me to go?" he asked softly.

She sat there, wondering how to answer that, and he finally moved so that he faced her, his body at an angle to hers. He put his hand on her shoulder, his arm brushing against her breast, sending an involuntary shudder through her body.

"Do you want me to go, Betsy?" he repeated softly.

There was a long moment when they locked eyes, then something shifted in the depths of his, and he was pulling her toward him, his mouth closing over hers.

He kissed her slowly, gently at first, and Betsy felt a response leaping up in her that surprised her with its intensity. Her arms went around his neck, drawing him closer to her so that she could feel her breasts being pressed against his hard chest. It felt so good, so right to be in his arms. She ran her hand through his shaggy hair, then drew his head still closer to hers. His tongue reached out and traced the outline of her lips, and she sighed and closed her eyes, her lips parting against his hungry mouth, which now seemed to want to devour her. She returned his kisses hungrily, wanting nothing more than to stay in his arms and be kissed by him. It had been so very long since her passions had been aroused, she had forgotten how exciting it could be.

He moved, pulling her over so that she lay across his lap, bending down so that his mouth never left hers. Then his tongue was in her mouth, exciting her. She could feel the passion in her body, long dormant, beginning to stir. She hadn't felt like this in years— too many years. She felt like a young girl being awakened for the first time as his lips made moaning sounds over hers and his hands moved gently up and down her back. One hand moved to cup a firm breast and caress it, and she could feel her nipple responding to his touch, blossoming beneath his hand. She arched her back, pressing her breast hard against his hand, urging him on, her own hands reaching beneath his sweater to move along his hard back and pull him even closer.

Their tongues were dueling as his hand reached beneath her sweater to find the clasp between her breasts. He unhooked it, and her large breasts burst forth from the restricting bra. His fingers moved from one nipple to the other, pulling at them, making them grow hard beneath his touch. She felt her body dissolving at his touch and she moved her legs up over the arm of the couch, curling her body around to his. She couldn't remember ever feeling so excited before or so vulnerable. She simply placed herself in his hands and let him take over.

And then it stopped.

His hand moved from beneath her sweater, his mouth lightly kissed her forehead, her eyelids, the tip of her nose, then he leaned his head back against the couch, looking down at her through half-closed lids. He brushed damp hair back off her forehead, straightened her sweater, then reached out and took a swallow of his brandy.

"What now, Betsy? Do you still want me to stay?" His voice was gruff, uneven.

She couldn't understand why he had stopped, why he was asking her questions. Could he turn his emotions on and off so easily? Her green eyes were glazed as she stared up at him wordlessly, her breathing ragged.

He gave a deep sigh. "You don't date, you don't want a relationship, you're not looking for a husband. You're independent and self-sufficient, or so you claim. What do you want from me?"

"I don't want anything from you," she said in a small voice.

"Then you'd be the first one. Every woman is after something." His voice was cynical, but his eyes were soft.

"I don't know what I want," she said, more to herself than to him. *Now,* she added silently. *I don't know what I want now.*

He lifted her up off his lap and set her back beside him on the couch. He lit a cigarette, then got up and put on his jacket. "Well, when you find out, honey, let me know."

She couldn't believe he could just stop like that. Just stop and get up and walk away. Why wasn't he staying? Didn't he want to make love to her? It had all been so perfect, and now he was destroying it by leaving. A small feeling of anger stirred within her. Well, she certainly wasn't going to beg him to stay. She had never begged *any* man to stay.

She got up and followed him to the door, where he was zipping up his jacket.

He leaned down and kissed her again, one hand lazily moving to cup one of her firm breasts. She could feel her nipple harden in response, sending electrical impulses through her body. She leaned against him, reaching up to encircle his neck with her arms, but he moved back, breaking off the kiss. His hand stayed on her breast, gently caressing it as he watched her reaction. "Is this what you want?"

I want you Nick, you, some part of her longed to cry out, to tell him that she loved him. She was sure it was in her eyes, plain to see, as she looked up at him. But some other part of her cautioned her against saying the words. *Protect yourself, Betsy,* it seemed to be saying. *Don't say it. Don't make yourself vulnerable to this man.*

His hand was insistent on her breast. "Is it, Betsy? Answer me. Is this what you want from me?"

She put her hand over his and shuddered. She did want it. She wanted his hands all over her, his mouth all over her. She wanted all of him, wanted him so badly, she couldn't speak.

He pushed her back against the door, pressing his body against hers so that she could feel the source of his own excitement hard against her. His mouth came down cruelly on hers in a harsh kiss that bespoke of no affection, only lust. Then just as abruptly he pulled away to leave her trembling, propped against the door for support.

"If it's sex you want, honey, any man could oblige you. In fact, I could name half a dozen at the office right now who'd be glad to serve your purpose."

She stood there, stung by his words, as he opened the door and stepped out into the hall.

"You're playing games with me, Betsy. Don't do that." His voice was deceptively calm but he slammed the door hard behind him, and she could hear him almost running down the stairs.

She locked the door and then just stood there unmoving. She wasn't even aware at first that she was crying, the tears running unheeded down her face. She couldn't remember the last time she had cried. Not when the house was sold, not even when Tom had asked for the divorce.

She cried soundlessly, vaguely aware of Jason sleeping in the next room. What she really wanted to do was rage and howl, run next door to Abby to be told that all men were cruel and heartless, that she shouldn't have let her feelings take control. That the magic formula was: NEVER TRUST A MAN. Because she had begun to trust Nick, to open herself up to him, to even fall in love with him, and he had betrayed that trust by exposing her vulnerability. He had left her feeling like a fool.

Mechanically she began to get ready for bed. Although she finished off both their glasses of brandy, sleep wouldn't come. She tossed and turned, still feeling Nick's hands on her, still remembering the taste of his kisses. Over and over she asked herself why he had changed so suddenly. Why something that was feeling so right to her could seem wrong to him, wrong enough to make him walk out the door, humiliating her with talk of other men. She couldn't understand it at all. Maybe she just didn't understand men. Maybe it was some inherent flaw in her that made the men she loved walk out on her. She had been just as shocked and confused when Tom had asked for a divorce as she had been tonight when Nick had so abruptly put an end to their lovemaking. Neither time had she had any forewarning as to what was about to happen.

Well, it had happened quickly, maybe she'd get over it quickly. Perhaps the next time she saw him, her feelings would have lessened, maybe even have gone completely. The early threads of love were fragile, tenuous; perhaps tonight's events would have severed them, and the next time she saw him she would feel nothing. And perhaps she was kidding herself.

Chapter Five

Nothing much happened on Sunday, except that the temperature dropped down to an unprecedented twenty-seven degrees, and Betsy snapped at Jason all day until finally, in a moment of guilt, she dragged him down to Macy's and bought him two new sweat shirts. One had the number sixteen on the back, and the other had NEW YORK YANKEES emblazoned across the front. Abby and Carla were visiting relatives in Brooklyn for the day, which meant that Betsy was left to do her fretting and fuming in obscurity.

On Monday night Betsy went to work determined to be very cool and very businesslike with the enigmatic Mr. Creme. This was thwarted, however, by the fact that he had left by the time she arrived. She found that Pete Beck had signed up for all of her time as well as Lisa's.

Betsy liked Lisa. She seemed the most intelligent of the actresses and was also the most successful. She had a business manager as well as an agent and frequently got work doing commercials and bit parts in soap operas. The two of them got cups of coffee and then sat down to wait for Mr. Beck to start handing out the work.

They spoke a little of the theater, a little more about the problems of finding a reasonably priced apartment in New York, and then, straight out of left field, Lisa said, "I hear you're seeing Nick."

Betsy was so surprised that she spilled her coffee right down the front of her white blouse, causing Lisa to laugh and say, "Well, I guess that answers my question."

"I'm not really seeing him," Betsy protested, wondering how in the world that rumor could have gotten started.

"Listen, it was obvious from the moment he started signing up for you. That's always the first clue with Nick. Also, someone saw you together at the Garden Saturday night."

So much for anonymity in the big city! "It wasn't a date; we just met there and sat together."

Lisa was looking highly amused. "It's no big deal, Betsy—we've all dated Nick at one time or another. And if you're worried about Christine, don't be; her three months are up."

"What three months?"

"You mean he hasn't spelled it out for you yet? He only dates a woman for three months. After that he figures she'll start to get serious, want to live with him or marry him, I suppose, and he breaks it off. Regular as clockwork—three months and *finito*!"

Betsy was staring at her in shock. "That's the most cold-blooded thing I ever heard."

"Listen, he's fair about it; always spells it out at the beginning of a relationship, so if the woman wants to forget about it, there's no hard feelings."

"That man should be shot!"

"Well, no one's ever said no to him yet. I think we

all saw it as a challenge—thought *we'd* be the one to change his mind, maybe get an extension. But no dice. Three months and Mr. Creme simply disappears, if you know what I mean.''

"Well, I'm not dating him and I don't intend to,'' Betsy said adamantly.

"Oh, you should—Nick's a lot of fun to date. Takes you to nice places and is a real gentleman. You usually end up good friends with him too, and Nick's not a bad friend to have. He always does my income taxes for me for nothing, saves me money, too.''

"In other words,'' said Betsy, "he doesn't want to get serious.''

"He's still hung up about his wife walking out on him. Still in love with her, I guess. There are some men like that, you know; they only fall in love with one woman in their life. Kind of romantic, if you think about it.''

Betsy didn't want to think about it. She didn't want to think about *any* of it. She wondered what she would have done if Nick had spelled out his three-month game plan to her. She supposed it would have depended on when he had told her. Before Saturday night she probably would have told him to get lost. But *during* Saturday night? That she couldn't be sure of. Probably, like the others, she would have accepted it and then ignored it, thinking that she'd be the exception to the rule. What bothered her most was that he had kissed her, even caressed her, and her three months hadn't even started. Probably her "seduction scene,'' as he had termed it, had thrown him off schedule. She supposed he didn't really explain the plan to a woman until he started dating her, and she and Nick had never actually dated.

She was glad when Mr. Beck started handing out the work so that she didn't have time to think about it anymore or have to answer more curious questions from Lisa. As soon as she got home, though, she sat down over coffee with Abby and brought her up to date.

"Yeah, I heard about that, but I never understood why any of the women put up with it," said Abby when Betsy told her about Nick's three-month plan.

"He never told *me* about it," said Betsy.

"Well, maybe you're the exception."

"Why would I be the exception?"

"You've got me, kid. But I'm sorry to see you've really fallen for the guy. I'm afraid you're just going to get hurt."

"That's already happened," said Betsy with a rueful smile. "Anyway, I think Nick and I have run our course, and in a lot less than three months. Actually, it's started and ended before the first date."

"I don't know, Betts—maybe you just need a man. It has been quite a while since Tom."

"I thought of that," Betsy admitted. "In fact, I wish it were true, but it's not. If I just needed a man, I would have been looking for one, but Nick had to practically hit me over the head to make me notice him. No, I really like him, Abby. He's intelligent and fun to be with and he. . . well, he makes me feel good. And Saturday night. . . I tell you quite honestly, that man moves me in ways Tom never did."

"Would you marry him?"

"He's no more interested in marriage than I am."

"That doesn't answer my question."

"It's academic anyway, Abby, since I won't be seeing him again unless he apologizes for Saturday night."

"I can't see Nick apologizing."

Betsy couldn't either, unfortunately.

She didn't see him again until Thursday night, when he had once again signed up for her. She went into his office, determined to play it very cool, only to be confronted with an even more businesslike attitude on his part. He was polite but curt when he handed her the work, then left the office for home before she finished it.

A certain spitefulness in her was glad to see that his cold seemed worse. There were cough medicine and cough drops in evidence on his desk, and his ashtray was spotlessly clean. If he wasn't smoking, his cold must really be bad.

Friday morning she was awakened early by an excited Jason, who was looking out the window and shouting, "It's snowing, Mom—it's snowing!"

She buried her head under the pillow. "It can't be snowing, Jason, it's too early in the season."

"Well, I think I know snow when I see it," he said in an affronted tone of voice.

She got out of bed and went to the window. Sure enough, all the roof gardens were covered with snow, and between two buildings she could see pedestrians scurrying along beneath umbrellas. She began to feel as excited as Jason; she too loved the first snow of winter, although by February she was generally sick and tired of it. And the greatest thing about snow in New York would be she'd never have a driveway to shovel!

It snowed steadily all day, and by the time she picked the children up from school the city seemed to be clearing out with people heading home early from their offices.

That night Nick again signed up for her. Most of the attorneys and paralegals had headed home early because of the hazardous road conditions, but a few who lived in Manhattan had stayed on. He was curt, almost to the point of brusqueness, with her when he handed her the work, and she noticed his voice was hoarse and his face flushed. *Suffer, Nicholas Creme,* she thought. *I'm not feeling all that great myself, and it's all due to you!*

During the evening attorneys with radios in their offices said the weather bureau was reporting five to seven more inches of snow before the storm slackened around midnight. Then word filtered down from the most senior partner that anyone who wished to leave early could do so. Gradually the offices emptied until, by ten, the place was practically deserted, the noise stilled, corridors vacant. Betsy stayed on, thinking she was probably the only one left. She knew she was one of the few who worked there who lived within walking distance. And she certainly didn't want to incur Nick's wrath by leaving his work unfinished.

She found him still in his office when she finished his work at midnight and took it in.

"Thanks for staying—I needed this to work on tomorrow," he growled, his hoarse voice sounding rather appealing.

She was looking past him out the window, where a curtain of snow was torn occasionally by heavy gusts. "You're welcome, Mr. Creme."

"I'm walking you home," he muttered.

"What?"

"You heard me. I'm walking you home. I know only a deranged mugger would be out there in weather like this, but I don't want to come in Monday morning and hear about your having been buried in a snowdrift."

Right. Just his responsibility to employees, that's all it was, she thought angrily. Anyway, he was in no condition to walk her home. He should be home in bed under an electric blanket, from the sound of that cold.

But she gave him merely a mild look. "I'll just turn off the machines and meet you back here," she said sweetly, then left his office.

She quickly closed the place down, put on her snow boots, buttoned up her storm coat, then headed straight for the elevators, where Nick was waiting, a sardonic look in his eyes.

"I can read you like a book, Betsy," he said as they headed down in the elevator.

Not quite like a book, she felt like saying. *Only on certain occasions, Mr. Creme. When it really matters, you read me totally wrong.*

Two feet out of the building they were almost blown away. This was not one of those soft, gentle snowfalls with big flakes drifting down slowly in silence and sparkling in the light of streetlamps and neon signs. This was a maelstrom. Snow came whirling straight down, was blown sideways, and even rose up in gusty puffs from drifts beginning to pile up on street corners.

He grabbed her arm and started down Lexington Avenue.

"Nick, you sound terrible. Why don't you go home to bed? I can get home all right—honestly."

"I'm taking you home." His tone was firm.

"But Nick—"

"Just keep quiet for once in your life and do what I say!"

She huddled against him as, bent over, they walked against the snow. After a block they looked like two snowmen trudging along, and she felt like something that had been left in the freezer. It took them four times longer to reach her building than it usually took, and when they got there he waited while she opened the door, then stepped into the entry hall with her.

He reached out, trying unsuccessfully to brush the snow from her hair, then put his hands on her shoulders and looked steadily into her eyes. "Look, Betsy, I'm sorry about some of the things I said to you Saturday night. Not *all* of them, mind you, but some of them."

He started to hug her, but she pushed him away. "*Which* things are you sorry about?"

He sighed and leaned back against the mailboxes, setting off the buzzers in several of the apartments. "About what I said about the other lawyers."

She waited, but that seemed to be it. She wanted him to say he was sorry he left her like that, but obviously he wasn't. Well, it was more of an apology than she had expected.

"Why didn't you tell me about your three-month-only policy?"

He looked startled for a moment, then smiled. "Oh, you heard about that?"

"It seems to be common knowledge." Half the women in the city had probably heard about it. Or participated in it.

"Well, for two reasons. One, it applies only to women I date, and we don't date, and two, it wouldn't be necessary with you even if we were dating. I hardly need to have any kind of policy if you neither date, have relationships, nor plan to re-marry, now, do I?"

Despite the logic of that she felt an urge to wipe the supercilious smile off his face. She muttered something she had taught herself in Arabic that week, but even to her own ears it sounded like gibberish.

"What was that?" he asked.

"Never mind."

"No, I want to know what you said."

"It was Arabic. I think it means your mother likes camels."

"My *mother* likes *camels*?"

"It's supposed to be an insult. I felt like swearing at you and that came to mind."

"I really don't understand you, Betsy. I apologize, and then you swear at me."

Betsy looked down at the floor. "I didn't much like your apology."

"Well, it's the best you're going to get."

"I don't like your three-month policy, either."

"You know what they say about people who live in glass houses," he countered.

"Well, if I'm never going to catch a husband by not dating, you're never going to catch a wife with your three-month policy."

"But you see, that's the point of it."

For no reason at all she felt so unaccountably angry with him that she muttered a good night and turned and started up the stairs. She half expected him to follow her or at least call out, but instead she heard the door slam, and when she turned around to look he had gone.

SHE PICKED UP THE PHONE on the first ring, only to hear a low, sibilant whisper that she couldn't understand. Good heavens, was she receiving her first lewd phone call? But surely not at nine thirty on a Saturday morning. She had heard they were usually middle-of-the-night occurrences.

But, just in case it was, she said in a very businesslike manner, "I'm sorry, but I can't understand you. However, if this turns out to be an off-color phone call, I must warn you that I intend to hang up and report it." There. That ought to nip it in the bud.

She could swear she heard a low laugh, then a deep, racking cough. She waited patiently for it to subside, then the whisper came again, this time more clearly. "Betsy? Don't hang up."

She looked at the phone and debated. If he knew her name, that made it much worse somehow. "Yes? Who is this?"

"Nick." It came out clear, then she heard more coughing.

"Is that you, Nick?"

"Yes. I've lost my voice. Can you understand me at all?"

"Yes, but if you've lost your voice, you shouldn't be talking, should you?"

"Please, it's an emergency."

"I really think you ought to get off the phone—"

"Betsy, please! I have to have that document you did for me last night, and no one showed up at work today because of the snow. Would you do me a very large favor?"

"You want me to pick it up and deliver it to you?"

"You could use a messenger service, but I doubt whether any of them are even open because of the weather."

"I don't mind doing it."

"I wouldn't ask, but I know how much you like walking around the city."

"I don't even know where you live."

"I'm on East Fifty-fourth. It's not that far from the office, but in the other direction from you. I'm in the phone book."

"You really shouldn't be talking so much, Nick."

"I really shouldn't keep walking people home in inclement weather."

She laughed. "Lucky for you the game's been called because of snow."

"I forgot about that. You mean if the game was on, you wouldn't do it?"

"That's right."

"Football's more important to you, huh?"

"More important than a document on tax shelters, yes."

"You can bring Jason along if you want."

"That's not necessary—he'll be thrilled to learn he can watch cartoons this morning. I think you ought to stop talking now, Nick. I'll see you soon."

"Hey, Betsy."

"Yes?"

"It's not a date."

She took Jason next door and explained to Abby, then started to bundle up in her warmest clothes: regular underwear; then a suit of long thermal underwear; two pairs of wool socks; a cotton turtleneck beneath a heavy, itchy wool sweater; a pair of ski pants; her down vest; a waterproof parka over it all; and ski mittens and a knit hat.

She looked at herself in the mirror, decided she looked like a moose, then further decided she didn't care. He had a pretty good idea of what she looked like beneath all those clothes, anyway.

She went downstairs and entered a white world. Snow was still falling softly, and everywhere she looked all she could see was white. Cars that had been left parked in the street were totally covered, only vague outlines showing what make they might be. There wasn't a bus, a taxi, any transportation of any kind to be seen. When she got to the corner of Lexington Avenue she saw people cross-country skiing down the middle of the street. It was a perfect white world, and she had never seen New York look so lovely. She was sorry the game had been called off. Central Park in the snow must be breathtaking, and playing football in the snow had the added attraction of the ground being soft when you were tackled.

She didn't even bother with the sidewalks, just walked straight up the middle of Lexington among the skiers, glad that Nick had given her the excuse to get out. She also had to admit to a curiosity about where and how he lived. She assumed it would be a typical bachelor's lair: modern walnut furniture or a lot of chrome and glass, a stereo, no doubt a well-stocked bar. She only hoped he wasn't so crass as to have a circular bed with a mirrored ceiling, but it was hard to tell what kind of taste men had. And, after last night, she was afraid she wouldn't see him again until work the following week. Which would have meant a long weekend thinking about him and wondering what he was doing. And whom he was doing it with.

She let herself into the office with her key. It was absolutely still. No one had gotten into work. She had heard on the radio that all transportation to the city was at a standstill.

She went into his office, picked up the document, and rolled it up in order to stick it into the nylon carryall she had brought along for that purpose. She wondered briefly if getting her over there with the document was some kind of ruse, but instantly dismissed the notion. When it came to work, Nick was all business, and if he said this was an emergency, it was.

She went out into the snow again, this time with anticipation. Maybe she should have brought Jason along; he would have loved dancing around in the snow, making snowballs, diving into the high drifts. Why hadn't it occurred to her to bring him? Surely he would have found it more exciting than watching cartoons, and he probably could have done that at Nick's apartment, anyway. And he was crazy about Nick. Had she wanted to visit Nick alone? In his apartment? She quickly dismissed that thought as ridiculous. Probably, somewhere in her sub-conscious, she hadn't wanted Jason exposed to Nick's cold. As for herself, she never caught colds.

When she arrived she found that he lived in a modern building with a doorman on duty. Which shouldn't have surprised her. After all, he was a suc-cessful attorney. The doorman announced her to Nick over an intercom, then she took a carpeted, music-filled elevator up to his floor.

A paler Nick than she had ever seen filled his door-way. He was unshaven, his hair looked like it hadn't seen a comb in days, and his large form was covered in blue pajamas and a warm-looking plaid wool robe. He looked utterly endearing to her at that moment. He gave her a halfhearted smile and motioned her inside—where she promptly got the shock of her life.

Here were the bright colors missing from out-doors. Red, green, yellow, blue, orange, purple, pink, all in chintz run wild. The couch, chairs, pil-lows, drapes, even the tablecloths covering the

numerous round tables, were flowers and birds, but-
terflies and rainbows. Wildly colored rugs covered
the floors; peonies ran rampant in the wallpaper.
Everything blazing and crawling. Overstuffed and
overwhelming! The room stunned the eye, shocked
the senses: a funhouse of wildly colored hues in
prints, stripes, checks, and plaids. She suddenly
found it difficult to breathe.

Nick was watching for her reaction. "I sublet it—
furnished," he finally croaked.

She was relieved to hear it.

He sat down on a plaid couch, instantly blending
into it. She chose a trellised chair.

"Shouldn't you be in bed?" she asked him.

He nodded, his face morose. He looked so pitiful,
she felt like hugging him.

"Can I make you anything, Nick? Tea? Coffee?"

He nodded.

"Which would you like?"

He shrugged.

She got up and removed her snow boots and then
her parka, hanging it on a hook she found by the
front door, a bright pink hook that blended into the
wallpaper. "Go back to bed, and I'll fix you some
tea."

She took the document out of the bag and handed
it to him. "Here, you can look at this while I fix you
something."

He nodded and got up, lumbering into the bedroom.

She found the kitchen and saw that not only did it
match the living room in decorating style, but it was

also immaculate. If her guess was right, Nick hadn't had a thing to eat. She looked in the refrigerator, saw enough ingredients for an omelet, and got to work.

Ten minutes later she entered the bedroom with tea, an omelet, and some buttered toast all arranged in rose-patterned plates on a white wicker tray. Outside snow, indoors a veritable flower garden!

She was used to it by now, and the fact that Nick was propped up in an old-fashioned brass bed with pink flowered sheets with lace on the edges didn't even faze her. She noted the dressing table in one corner with the ruffled skirt, the white shutters on the windows, the framed flower prints on the wall, and the rocking chair with ruffled pillows in one corner. It was like the ultimate in little girls' bedrooms in a decorating book. Not the kind she had ever fancied having, as she had been something of a tomboy, but she could remember friends with similar rooms. The only thing missing was the doll on the bed. Instead there was Nick, looking more like a well-loved teddy bear than a doll.

He looked hungrily at the tray as she set it across his lap, tried to say something and failed, then wrote on the back of one of the document pages and held it up for her to see. "Thank you for the food—I sublet from an interior decorator."

She supposed it was possible. "Just eat your food," she ordered him, sitting down in the rocker with a cup of tea to keep him company.

The big hulk of a man looked so incongruous among the frilly pink sheets that she had to smile. She wondered that the women he brought here didn't find the decor ludicrous and tell him so, but obviously they didn't care. Or maybe he just didn't care about their opinions. She was only glad she didn't have to live in the place. She was sure it would make her claustrophobic.

She sat in silence while he ate the food on the tray. It was so very still in his apartment; no sound anywhere except the occasional clink of his fork against the plate. She realized it was partly due to there being no traffic in the streets, not even an occasional airplane going by overhead. She told him about the world outside, the all-white world, and how people were skiing down the middle of the streets and how the snowdrifts had buried the parked cars.

Then she settled back in silence again and watched him as he finished. Despite the background of pink he looked utterly masculine in his blue pajamas, his dark face made even darker by the growth of beard. His blue pajamas were silky and cool-looking, and she wondered what it would feel like to be pressed up against him. She felt herself flush, then looked up from his chest to see his eyes on her, almost as though he knew what she was thinking. He took the last sip of his tea, then licked his lips, his eyes still locked with hers.

The room suddenly felt stifling hot, and Betsy got up to take the tray, avoiding his eyes, then went to the kitchen and cleaned up the few dishes she had dirtied. She'd have to go now, she supposed. She had brought him the document, fixed him some food— there wasn't really anything more she could do. But she didn't want to leave. She wouldn't see him again until work, which would leave the whole weekend to sit home and think about him. And the night before he had been angry with her when he left. She didn't want to leave him feeling that way again. To be honest, she didn't want to leave him at all.

She went back to his bedroom and stood by his bed for a moment, looking down at him. The top button of his pajamas was undone, and she could see the thick mat of dark hair curling on his chest. How could a man look feverish and sick and so damn sexy all at the same time?

"Well, I guess I'll be going, then," she said diffidently, her hands in the pockets of her ski pants, her face looking more forlorn than she would have wished.

He reached out a hand to her, and she took it, noticing how warm it felt. She put her other hand on his forehead, much as she would do with Jason when he was sick. He *did* feel awfully warm, but then so did she. The apartment itself was very warm, unlike her building, where it depended on the whim of the super whether they got heat or not and at what hours, and his whims were erratic at best. But she was wearing a lot of clothes, and Nick was wearing practically nothing.

He pulled her down until she was sitting on the bed next to him. "Is there anything else you want, Nick?"

His fingers were moving across her wrist. He nodded.

"Do you want me to bring the TV set in here for you? There should be some college games on today that you could watch."

He shook his head.

"Do you need anything from the store? I have time if you want me to run out."

He shook his head more decisively this time.

He was looking at her in a way that seemed to make her melt. "Just tell me what you want, Nick," she said, her voice sounding ragged to her ears.

Slowly, deliberately, he pulled her down toward him, his eyes never leaving hers, until she was leaning on top of his chest. Then his mouth sought her lips. She felt his rough, unshaven face against her own as his hard lips explored the softness of hers, pushing them apart and forcing her acceptance. An acceptance willingly given. She made a little sound of happiness against his mouth and moved closer against him. She wished she could feel the hardness of his chest against hers, but that was an impossibility, due to the layers of clothes she was wearing. His fingers wound in her hair and clenched tightly as his hungry mouth ravished hers. She could feel her body of its own volition move up on the bed beside him, her arms snaking their way around his neck. She thought she could hear his heart hammering in his chest beneath the thickness of her down vest. Or maybe that was her own heart she felt beating.

When his hands reached down and drew her body on top of his, she opened her eyes briefly to see the naked flame of passion in his. *I love you, oh, how I love you,* she told him silently, then sighed and lost herself again in his kisses. His hands were moving over her body, but she could barely feel them as he struggled to undo her vest. She raised her chest off his and let him unzip it, then pulled out of it and tossed it on the floor. She could feel him a little better now as one of his hands moved to cover her breast, instantly triggering some response in her that made her begin to move her hips sensuously against his own, causing him to groan and then respond in kind. Feeling wrapped in a warm, silent cocoon with him, she couldn't remember ever feeling so peaceful and so aroused at the same time.

Then he was trying to lift her sweater off and having a hard time of it, so she sat up, straddling him, while she pulled it over her head. He looked surprised to see the turtleneck beneath, and motioned for her to remove it, too. When she did, revealing her long underwear, he just shook his head in resignation.

"Did you feel you needed so much protection against me?" he said softly, his voice a bare croak.

"Maybe," she murmured softly, her hands going to his pajama-top buttons, undoing them and pulling the top apart so that she could lean down and nestle her head in his chest's furry covering. She kissed his chest until he pushed her back up and began to pull at the top of her thermal underwear, and she reached down and brought that too, over her head. Then she reached behind her and unhooked her lacy bra so that her breasts were free and loose above him. He looked at them in wonder, reached out, and then stopped, his eyes going to hers.

"Take everything off," he said softly. "I want to see your body."

Usually shy about people seeing her unclothed, she found herself feeling very differently now. She stood beside the bed and hurriedly unzipped her ski pants and let them fall to her feet, revealing her long, curved legs and rounded hips. Then she took off her long underwear and last the thin bikini panties she wore beneath it all. When at last she stood there naked, his eyes devouring her body, she found she didn't feel self-conscious as she thought she would. He seemed to approve of all her curves and looked at her as though he couldn't get enough of them. Then he threw back the blanket, and she got into bed beside him.

"You have an incredible body," he murmured to her as he moved to cover her body with his, his mouth once more going to hers as his hands explored her curves. He seemed to know exactly how and where to touch her to bring out her responses. Waves of ecstasy flowed through her body at each touch, and when he moved off of her, she reached out for him, wanting to pull him back, but he looked down at her, shaking his head, then moved his mouth to one of her breasts. As his tongue found one hard nipple she groaned and arched her back, then sank back on the mattress, willing him to do what he wished.

His mouth on her breasts, first one and then the other, aroused her to a feverish pitch. Her hands went to his head, trying to bring him even closer to her, wanting to be devoured by his hunger. One hand was cupping her breast, his teeth gently nibbling on it, the other was on the inside of her thigh, caressing it gently, up and down, until she thought she would go wild, so deep was her longing for him. "Yes,

Nick," she murmured over and over. "Yes, Nick, oh, yes."

When he moved further down she gasped with pleasure before losing herself to the touch of his mouth, his tongue. Slowly and skillfully he began raising her to the heights of ecstasy. She found herself clutching the sides of the bed as all control vanished and she was gradually brought to that place where she found herself hovering on a precipice, dizzying waves of rapture engulfing her frenzied body, and then she was spiraling off into space, conscious only of being transported further than she'd ever been. Waves of shock shuddered through her body as he lifted his head and rested it on her trembling stomach.

Gradually she became aware of her surroundings and her hands went to his head, smoothing back his tousled hair, then trying to pull him up to her. He moved beside her and took her in his arms, his lips gentle on her temple as they clung together. She felt more love for him at that moment than she had ever felt for Tom. In retrospect Tom had been a selfish lover, seeking only to satisfy himself. Never had he made her feel that her body was a precious vessel, worthy of admiration.

Nick raised himself on one elbow and looked down at her, his eyes traveling the length of her body and then back to her shining face. "You are so very beautiful," he whispered softly, "as I knew you would be."

"I could afford to lose a few pounds," said Betsy shyly, unused to compliments about her body.

"No, not an ounce—you're absolutely perfect." His hand gently caressed one breast, then he leaned down and kissed it. "You were just what the doctor ordered, you know that?"

She reached to pull him down on top of her, wanting him to be fulfilled the way she had been, but he shook his head.

"I'm too doped up with cold medicine, I'm afraid."

"You mean it wasn't only your voice you lost?" she teased him.

He nodded ruefully.

"But don't you mind?"

He gave her a warm smile. "How could I possibly mind being given the chance to make love to you? There will be other times, I promise you that."

She looked at him in wonder, her eyes wide, and he laughed. "Didn't your husband ever make love to you like that?"

She shook her head.

"Then he was a fool!"

Betsy was thinking it was Nick's wife who was the fool. If it had been Nick she was married to, she wouldn't have given him up without a fight.

"Did you like it?"

Her face dissolved into a look of contentment as she nodded. She had loved it; she loved him, but she couldn't say the words. She moved her head to rest it on his comfortable chest, and his arm around her tightened.

"What am I going to do with you, Betsy? I don't know what you want from me, whether it's just the sex.... All I know is we seem to be getting pretty close for not even dating.''

"I just don't know what I want, Nick.''

He moved down beside her on the bed, one arm flung out behind his head. "*Is* it just the sex?''

"No.''

"Do you like being with me?''

A pause. "Most of the time.''

He chuckled at that. "Do you want to start dating?''

"No!'' she said emphatically. That was something she definitely did not want to do. Starting to date would mean starting the three-month-only plan, and she didn't even want to think about that.

"Does that mean you don't want to see me again?''

She turned toward him. "Of course I want to see you again.''

He gave a deep sigh, then there was a long silence. Finally, "I don't know, Betsy; I hear the words but I don't hear the music.''

The music's in my heart, she thought, *a whole symphony of sounds, and all of them saying I love you, Nick. But you're probably very used to hearing women say that to you, while you say nothing at all. Nothing. And your silence is stilling my heart.*

She turned to look at him and saw that his eyes were closed and his breathing even. He was sound asleep, looking as peaceful as Jason when she'd go in at night to cover him up.

She got quietly out of bed and put her clothes back on. She went into the bathroom and combed her hair, noticing the redness on her face from his prickly chin. When she got back to the bedroom she covered him with the blanket, then saw that the phone beside the bed was off the hook and wondered if it had happened while they were making love.

She put it back on and it immediately rang. She looked at Nick, but the sound didn't seem to be penetrating his sleep, so she picked it up and said a soft hello.

"Is Nicky there?" The voice was throaty, definitely sexy. And most definitely female.

"Yes, he is—do you want me to waken him?"

A moment of silence. "He's *sleeping*? In the middle of the afternoon?"

"I think it's the cold medicine he's been taking."

"Nick's sick?"

"Pretty bad—he's lost his voice." Then, thinking she really ought to explain her presence, "I had to bring over some papers for him from the office."

"Oh. Well, I guess that means our date is off for tonight. Will you leave him a message and say that Janine called?"

"I certainly will," replied Betsy, hanging up the phone in a controlled fury.

She wrote the message down on the back of a document page, propped it against the phone, then quickly left the apartment. So, he was going to go straight from having her in his bed to another woman that night. Who no doubt would be glad to warm his bed once again.

She barely noticed that the snow had stopped when she got outside his building. She was glad she had said she didn't want to date him. He knew very well she wasn't seeing any other men, but *he* was seeing half the female population of New York! Which was probably why he was so damn proficient at making love! Maybe Tom hadn't been so exciting in bed, but at least he was a one-woman man.

Why, oh, why, had she been so foolish as to fall in love with the Don Juan of Midtown?

Chapter Six

On Sunday the temperature rose to forty and a steady rain was falling, turning the white wonderland into a drab city filled with gray slush. The weather fitted her mood, Betsy decided. She wondered who was administering to Nick's needs today. Janine? Some other woman? *Numerous* women?

In a flurry of hyperactivity she banished Jason from his room and gave it a thorough cleaning. Then she attacked the living room, the kitchen, and the bathroom. As the place was small, she was finished well before noon with the rest of the day looming in front of her. It was too wet to take Jason out, there wasn't enough to keep him occupied, and she just couldn't seem to get her thoughts off Nick.

She finally settled down with *The New York Times* crossword puzzle. If she listed everything in the world she hated, that crossword puzzle would head the list. Before coming to New York she had *never* had trouble doing one. With this one she was lucky to end up getting fifteen words.

She was staring at it with revulsion when Abby stopped by to suggest they take the kids to the Disney movie playing on Thirty-fourth Street. Jason was overjoyed when she agreed. As for her, she was glad of any excuse not to have to work on that puzzle. Even a Disney movie was a better idea.

After ten minutes of the movie, though, Abby and Betsy were squirming in their seats and casting surreptitious glances at each other. The movie was clearly as boring as staying home and staring at bare walls. When Abby said "Why don't we wait for them in the bar next door," Betsy didn't have to be asked twice. They told the children where to meet them, crawled over countless small bodies, and breathed a collective sigh of relief when they got outside.

They dived into Brew's next door. Outside a wild wind hooted faintly while rain drove relentlessly against the windows. Inside the air had been breathed too many times, but it was warm, dry, and, best of all, Disney characters weren't prancing around on a screen. They went to the back and found a table and grinned at each other like two kids let out of school early.

A waitress with an awesome bosom came by, and they ordered a bottle of wine and croissants, daring her to make any comment about the combination.

"This is the only civilized way to spend a Sunday in New York," said Abby after taking her first long swallow of the wine.

"Sitting in a bar?"

"No, getting drunk. The worst thing about being single is Sundays."

Betsy generally liked Sundays, but today she was inclined to agree. "What did you do on Sundays when you were married?"

Abby thought for a moment. "Got drunk. What did you do?"

"This time of year we usually watched football games."

"God, that's worse than getting drunk."

"Well, we used to drink beer while we watched them. Anyway, I like football. I think it's what I miss most about being married. We'd always bet on the games and pick different teams to cheer for.... I haven't seen a game since." Oh, dear—now she was getting nostalgic, and they certainly didn't need that on an already dreary day.

"Betts, you can come watch the games on my TV anytime."

Betsy smiled at her friend. "Oh, Abby—I know it would be just as boring for you as watching a Disney movie. Anyway, *I'm* the one who chose not to have a television set."

Abby leaned back in her chair and gave Betsy a mischievous look. "So, what's happening with Nick? Anything exciting happen yesterday? I have a certain sneaking suspicion you're holding back on me."

Betsy felt herself flush and hoped the dimness of the bar concealed it. It didn't.

"Aha! Now, let me guess. You went over to visit the sick man in his apartment, and he looked so adorable in his ski pajamas that you seduced him. Am I right?"

It was so close to the truth, Betsy had to laugh. "They weren't ski pajamas. Actually, I think they were silk. But Abby, wait until you hear about his apartment."

Abby shook her head. "Oh, no—it's not his apartment I want to hear about."

But Abby heard about it anyway, in minute detail, and also heard about a few other things. Betsy had a fleeting thought of Nick confiding in his friends the way she confided in Abby, but then dismissed it from her mind. She'd never know about it, anyway.

Abby was shaking her head in wonder. "That sure doesn't sound like your everyday bachelor pad. But, whatever the decor, it seemed to work on you."

"That man would get to me in *any* decor. And has," said Betsy.

Abby grabbed the fourth croissant before Betsy could devour it along with the previous three. "So what's happening now? I take it you two are at least dating."

Betsy shook her head, watching as Abby slowly enjoyed the pastry. "No, I don't want to date him."

"That doesn't make any sense at all. You want to make love with him, but you don't want to date him?"

Betsy realized how ridiculous it sounded. "I just don't want to be one of his three-month women, Abby. And that reminds me, who's Janine?"

"I don't know any Janine."

Betsy told her about the phone call. "Anyway, as long as we're not dating, I'm at least different from the others."

"That's just semantics, Betsy. If you're seeing him, that's the same as dating him. The only difference is you're missing out on going places. I don't see where *that* gets you."

"We went to the Garden," Betsy said. "Besides, he thinks every woman wants something from him; I want to be different."

"But you *do* want something from Nick."

"Why do I have to agree to some three-month deal when I'm in love with him?"

"Maybe you'll be the exception."

"Right now I'm the exception. If I agree to that, I'll just be joining all the others."

"What *do* you want from him, Betsy?"

"That's what he keeps asking me."

"Well, it's a good question. What do you want, six months? A year? What?"

"I guess I just want to be able to see him as long as I'm in love with him."

"And what if that's forever?"

Betsy gave her a stunned look. She had never projected it that far in the future. "I don't know. I guess I'd want to see him forever, then."

"Betsy, my love, it sounds to me like you are talking about marriage."

"No, I *don't* want to marry him. I never want to get married again."

"It wouldn't have to be like it was with Tom."

"*Tom?* Why, Nick's a hundred times the philanderer Tom was. Tom wasn't running around; he simply fell in love with another woman and did what he thought was right in the circumstances."

Abby was shaking her head. "There's a vast difference, Betts. Nick isn't married. It's quite accepted for single men to run around, you know. There's no reason why *you* couldn't be dating several men. Which might not be a bad idea, actually.''

"I don't want to date other men. I love him. Damn it, Abby, why did he have to do this to me? I was perfectly happy until he started hounding me. He *made* me fall in love with him, just as though he'd set out to do it. And it happened so fast! It took me ages to fall in love with Tom, but with Nick it was practically overnight.''

"Love at first sight. That's romantic,'' Abby mused.

"It was *not* love at first sight. I couldn't stand him at first. Oh, I thought he was good-looking, sexy, but I certainly didn't like his attitude. I *still* don't like his attitude.''

"All I can say is that man has a potent charm. I don't know what it is about him, but he attracts women like flies.''

"Yes, and in three months he exterminates them,'' Betsy said with bitterness. "What am I going to do, Abby?''

Abby, obviously thinking it was required, asked for another bottle of wine. "Well, I'll tell you what I think. I think you're terrific, the absolutely finest person I know. And Nick's a damn fool if he doesn't see that. But the man's no fool; he's highly intelligent, so maybe he does see it and maybe he'll be different with you. But, based purely on his track record, I'd say maybe you ought to stop right now. I know you're going to be hurt, but if it keeps going on you'll probably be hurt a lot more later.''

"But then I'd have to go on seeing him every night in the office. I don't know if I could handle that."

"You could always quit. You've been trained now; there's plenty of jobs for word processors."

Betsy looked across at her in indignation. "Quit my job over a *man*? Never!"

Abby chuckled. "That's my girl talking. Keep them in their proper perspective, I always say."

"You always cheer me up, Abby."

"What are friends for?"

When the children arrived they were forced to listen to a detailed description of the film, just what they'd hoped to avoid by leaving it. They decided to stay and have dinner in the bar, and they all ordered roast beef and baked potatoes, the good warm meal cheering Betsy up even more.

When they got home she washed Jason's hair, read him a few chapters of *Tom Sawyer* while it dried, then got him into bed. She put the newspaper and the magazine in the trash, not even wanting to see that crossword puzzle again, then got undressed herself and opened the couch. She took out her Arabic book, planning on doing some studying, but instead went over the conversation she had had with Abby.

Her friend was right. She should break it off with Nick now before her life was hopelessly entangled with his. Sure she loved him, but she had loved Tom too, and gotten over it. As for having to see him at the office, she'd simply be so cool and remote that he'd finally give up and go after someone else. And it was just possible that he felt the challenge was over anyway after yesterday. Some men just liked to see if they could get a woman, and then after they had her...But that didn't even bear thinking about. She just couldn't believe that of him. Or of herself for being so foolish.

Yes, that would be the game plan. She would be cool with Nick at work. Distant. It might not even be a bad idea to take up flirting—with the other attorneys, of course. But then *they* might ask her out, and she didn't want that. She could even hint to Nick that she preferred women, that she and Abby had something going...No, he'd never believe that. Certainly not after Saturday. But Nick had an ego like every other man; he would only take her coolness so long and then he'd turn elsewhere. So be it. She wanted her peace of mind back again, and that meant getting rid of Mr. Nicholas Creme.

She opened up her Arabic book and began to study. She could read a little now, and even write a little, but as for speaking it, she had no idea if she was getting the pronunciation right. It would probably be better not to even try that until she got into class, for fear of creating bad habits.

The telephone rang, startling her. Hoping it wasn't Tom again, she picked it up with misgivings.

"How are you doing?"

Oh, no—and just when she thought she had put him from her mind. His voice seemed to have returned, but it still had enough of a rasp in it to make it sound extremely sexy. Well, she was just going to have to become immune to that, and the time to start was now.

"I see your cold's better." That's the way, just keep it impersonal.

"Ummm. I told you—you were just what the doctor ordered."

Oh, no—she very much hoped he wasn't going to talk about yesterday. Just hearing his voice brought back memories of it, bringing an unexpected warmth to her body. *Be cool,* she ordered herself. *Be very cool.*

"Well, I'm glad to hear you're better."

"What did you do today? I tried to call you earlier, thought you might like to come over and watch the football games with me. In bed."

She wasn't going to think about that for one second. "Oh, we took the kids to a movie, but it was dreadful, so Abby and I ended up in a bar while the kids stayed and watched."

"I wish I'd been there with you. Did you talk about me?"

What a monumental ego! "No, we have better things to talk about."

He chuckled, obviously not believing her. "Why'd you leave like that? You didn't even leave a note."

"Oh, didn't you see the message by the phone?"

A pause. "Janine's an old friend I go to concerts with occasionally."

Oh, sure—an old friend with a very sexy voice. "I'm sure she is," said Betsy sardonically.

"Do I detect a note of jealousy in your voice?"

"*Jealousy?* Don't be ridiculous. Why should *I* care how many women you're seeing? *I'm* not dating you, thank God."

"Come on, Betsy—don't be like that. She *is* an old friend."

"How can she be an *old* friend, Nick? You only see them for three months!"

There was a silence. "Betsy, why are you doing this? Yesterday was beautiful. Why are you trying to ruin it?"

Feeling the tears threaten, Betsy spoke rapidly, hoping to get it all out before she broke down. "It's all over, Nick. As far as I'm concerned, once with any man is enough. After that the thrill is gone and it's all downhill." She hung up quickly before the enormity of the words sunk in, then took the phone off the hook in case he tried to call back.

She sat there in a daze, wondering where the words had come from. Once with a man was enough? There had only been Tom and Nick, and she certainly didn't believe once was enough with Nick. But *he* might believe it. And he'd hate it. After all, once with a man was even more devious than his three-month policy. Maybe it would teach him a well-deserved lesson. At the very least it ought to make him mad enough not to ever bother her again.

Abby would be proud of her. Abby would laugh when she heard what Betsy had said to the redoubtable Mr. Creme. And maybe she'd be able to laugh along with Abby, but she couldn't laugh now because she was crying too hard. She knew she had to do it; she knew it was to prevent herself from getting more hurt later. But it wasn't easy. It certainly wasn't easy.

IT WAS STILL RAINING ON MONDAY, the sky a uniform gray. Betsy stayed in. She tried to study but couldn't concentrate, picked up and put down books, and even found herself wishing she hadn't cleaned yesterday so she'd have something to do.

At one o'clock, in sheer desperation, she let herself into Abby's apartment and sat down to watch a soap opera. After listening to ten minutes of dialogue between star-crossed lovers, she gave up in disgust. She donned her raincoat and went out to get some air.

Walking aimlessly through Murray Hill, she passed the Bide-A-Wee below First Avenue, then went back and looked in the window. Maybe a kitten was just what they needed. Heaven knows, Jason could probably use something cheerful around the house; she certainly hadn't been lately.

She pushed open the door and went inside. It didn't turn out to be as easy to adopt a kitten as she had anticipated. There were forms to be filled out, even references to be given. But when she finally exited the place she was loaded down with a plastic cat box, a bag of litter, several cans of cat food, and an angry black kitten howling inside the cardboard carrying case they had provided—which Betsy fervently hoped wouldn't disintegrate in the rain.

Once home, she arranged the cat box under the bathroom sink and filled it with litter, then opened up the carrying case. The cat got in several scratches as she showed it the cat box and let it feel the sand with its paws. Then she set him down and got out of her wet clothes.

She could hear the kitten crying and looked around to locate the noise. He was perched precariously on top of the curtain valance, which he had reached by climbing up the curtains, leaving several holes in his wake. She couldn't reach him, couldn't coax him down. Finally she dragged a chair over and stood on it, but when she reached out to grab him, he ran to the other end of the valance. She got off the chair, moved it down beneath the kitten, and tried again. They repeated that little a cappella ballet several times before she gave up and went to pick the children up from school.

She hinted to Jason on the way home that she had a surprise for him. When they entered the apartment, the kitten was in the same spot but had stopped crying.

"Where's the surprise?" asked Jason, looking around the kitchen for perhaps some unexpected goodies to eat.

Betsy pointed up.

"Oh, wow—a cat!" yelled Jason. He marched over to the window and ordered the cat down. With what Betsy would swear was a knowing look, the cat glanced at her, then jumped down and went straight to Jason.

"Is he a boy, Mom?" Jason asked.

"Yes, he is."

"What's his name?"

"He hasn't got one. You can name him."

"I'm naming him Nick," announced Jason.

"No, you're *not* naming him Nick."

"If he was *my* cat, I'd name him Gypsy," offered Carla.

"That's a stupid name," muttered Jason. "His name is going to be Blacky, okay, Mom?"

Betsy nodded. It was an improvement over Nick, anyway.

Carla took her tie out of her jacket and began to walk around trailing it behind her. The kitten was falling all over himself trying to catch the string, causing fits of laughter from the children. They were so enthralled with Blacky, they didn't even ask to watch television.

Abby arrived home, duly admired the kitten, and Betsy set off for work.

Any hopes of not having a run-in with Nick were dashed when she saw that he had once more signed up for her time. She spent a few minutes in the washroom, combing her hair, went to the kitchen for coffee, and even chatted with the other night workers for a while. Anything to prolong the moment.

He was leaning back in his desk chair, hands clasped behind his neck, when she entered. His eyes were unfathomable as he handed her the work.

"It's rather long; you may have to stay late," he told her, his voice sounding back to normal.

She nodded, avoiding his eyes.

"I wouldn't be at all surprised if you end up the last to leave," he continued.

She looked out the window, concentrating on the rain.

"You do understand what I'm saying, Betsy, don't you?"

She looked at him then. He looked so handsome in a dark blue suit and white shirt, his tie loosened at the neck. If the desk wasn't between them, she'd be tempted to run into his arms and forget about anything but just being near him. But for *three* months?

something inside her asked. Her resolve strengthened. "Yes, Nick—I understand."

"Good, then I'll see you later," he said dismissively.

Betsy worked faster on that document than she had ever worked. When George finished early and offered to help, she gave him a stack of pages that she could supercopy onto her document when he had finished. She didn't stop for coffee, for talk—even for a visit to the washroom. Under ordinary circumstances it would have taken her well past midnight, but her fingers were flying across the keys with a strong determination to get out of there with the others and not be left alone with Nick. Because alone with him, she didn't think she could trust herself.

George's help was a godsend. It shaved off at least an hour's work, and by eleven thirty she was running off the document on the final printer with only a few pages left to go.

"Almost finished?" asked Lisa.

"I just have to wait for this document to print," Betsy told her.

"I'll take it off for you," Lisa offered. "I have one printing right after yours I have to wait for, anyway. Who's it for?"

"Nick."

"Go on, then—there's no sense in both of us having to stay. I'll take it in to him."

"Thanks, Lisa," said Betsy, feeling like throwing her arms around the girl and kissing her. What a relief; by the time Nick found out she had left, she'd already be safely at home.

"That kitten's more entertaining than a sit-com," said Abby when she went to pick up Jason. "When he grows up, we'll just get another one and our problem of entertaining the kids will be solved."

Betsy didn't get much sleep that night. Ten percent of the loss of sleep was due to wondering what kind of retribution Nick would have in store for her the following night. The other ninety percent was due to Blacky, who abandoned Jason and insisted on sleeping next to Betsy's face all night.

The sun was out in the morning for the first time in days. After taking the kids to school, Betsy came back to the apartment, thinking the kitten would keep her amused all morning. Blacky, however, had other ideas; he was making up for lost sleep, curled in a tight ball on Jason's unmade bed. Betsy left him there undisturbed and looked in *The Times* to see if anything was going on at the Security Council that morning. There was a discussion on apartheid in South Africa again, and she decided she'd go and sit in on it.

She left her building, crossed east, then turned north on First Avenue. She reached the UN building in about twelve minutes. She was such a regular by this time, the guards all knew her, and she took her usual seat in the center. There weren't many people there, just a few scattered tourists from the looks of it, which made it all the more surprising when someone slid into the seat beside her. She was concentrating on the speaker and didn't even look around; she just felt a little annoyed at her invasion of privacy.

"Let's get out of here, I want to talk to you," someone whispered in her ear, and her startled eyes flew to the right to see Nick seated beside her.

"Go away and leave me alone," she hissed, putting on her headset and turning up the volume. It was tuned in to Russian, but she was too upset to care.

He plucked the headset off her head and fastened his hand around her wrist. "Unless you want to cause an international incident, I suggest you get up and come quietly."

She turned furious green eyes on him. "How dare you come in here and order me around. I'm going to call one of the guards if you don't leave me alone."

There was a dangerous glint in his eyes as he reached for his wallet and extracted a card, flashing it in front of her eyes for her to read. "Now, who do you think they're going to believe, Betsy? An official for the IRS or you?"

With visions of him claiming to be arresting her for income tax evasion, thus ruining her reputation with the guards, Betsy got up resignedly from the seat and followed him out.

Once outside, Betsy turned to him in a fury. "What are you doing with that phony card, anyway?" she spat at him.

"It's not phony," he said mildly. "I just never bothered to turn it in. I figured it would come in handy one day. And I was right."

He sounded so self-satisfied, she wanted to kick him. "How'd you know I was there?"

"I took a chance. You said you enjoyed going there."

"Well, now that you've ruined my morning, you can just take off!"

He chuckled. "You try so hard to get rid of me, Betsy, and it's just no use. When are you going to learn that?"

"When are *you* going to learn I don't want to see you. Anywhere! Ever!"

His eyes looked amused. "I'll tell you what, Betsy. Why don't we go over to your apartment, and then you can tell me that again. And if you can, then I promise to leave you alone."

"You're not coming anywhere near my apartment," fumed Betsy.

"What are you afraid of, Betsy?"

"I'm not afraid of anything. I just don't want to be with you, that's all."

"We both know that all I'd have to do is just touch you, that's all, just touch you, and it would be a whole other ball game."

"Well, you're not going to touch me, and the ball game's over, Mr. Creme. If you don't quit harassing me, I'll just have to quit my job and work someplace else."

He stared at her in silence for a moment. "Is that what I'm doing? Harassing you?" His voice was hard.

She nodded.

His face suddenly looked older, tired. He looked up at the sky, running his hands through his hair, then looked back down at her. "I apologize, Ms. Miller. I won't harass you again." He turned and walked off. She stood watching him, sure that he'd turn around, come back for the next round. But he kept on walking until finally he just blended into the crowds...and she could no longer see him.

Well, she had won. She should feel exultant, but she didn't. She turned to go back inside the UN, then changed her mind. Apartheid no longer interested her. Nothing interested her. She turned and headed for home, her hands in her pockets, her head bent against a nonexistent wind.

Chapter Seven

When the phone rang at ten on the Saturday morning of Thanksgiving weekend, Betsy poked an arm out from her warm cocoon of blankets and picked up the receiver. She cradled it next to her ear on the pillow and mumbled a bleary hello.

"Betsy? Are you awake?"

She thought about it for a moment. "No."

"This is Nick."

Now she was awake. "Nick?"

"Hello, Betsy. Listen, I know what a terrible imposition this is on a holiday weekend, but I wonder if you could spare me an hour this morning. I wouldn't ask, but it's a real emergency. I have to get something typed, and everyone's off today."

Maybe it was a dream, she thought, pulling the covers up over her head to keep out the cold air. Nick couldn't really be calling her; not after all this time.

"Betsy? Are you still there? I tried everyone else first, but no one's around, or at least not answering their phones."

Her first impulse was to say no, but then she realized if any of the other partners had asked, she wouldn't hesitate a moment. It *was* her job, after all.

"Look, Betsy, I'll be glad to authorize triple time for you."

She stretched beneath the covers, feeling stiff from the cold. "No, it's not the money," she told him. "Abby's away for the weekend, and I don't know what I'd do with Jason."

"No problem. Bring him along. He can play with one of the machines while you're working; kids love those machines—they think they're computer games."

"What time do you want me?"

"Take your time. I'll be here when you get in. And thanks, Betsy—I really appreciate it."

She climbed reluctantly out of bed and walked over to the radiator under the window. Not a sign of heat. Out the window it was gray, the sky lowery, a hard wind blowing debris and pedestrians along. And probably no colder than in here, Betsy thought wryly.

She went into the bathroom and turned on the radio. An obscenely cheerful voice reported a storm front moving in from the west, with a dropping barometer and plunging thermometer. She turned it back off; that wasn't what she wanted to hear.

She looked into the mirror and didn't like what she saw. She had lost weight in the last few weeks, but instead of it coming off her hips, which she wouldn't have minded, the loss seemed to have centered on her face. Her cheeks had a hollow look, and there were dark smudges beneath her eyes. Somehow, since that day at the UN with Nick, she hadn't had much of an appetite.

At least the water heater seemed to be working. She took a long hot shower, hoping it would compensate for the lack of heat. She dressed in knee socks, corduroy pants, a thick white cable-knit sweater, and her Frye boots. She put on a little lip gloss to keep her lips from getting chapped, brushed her hair in a rather desultory way, then went in to rouse Jason from his bed.

"Why do I have to get up?" he complained, mirroring her own thoughts.

"Because I have to go in to work for an hour, and you're coming with me."

His eyes opened. "I get to see where you work?"

She had never thought he was interested. "Sure, you can even work one of the word processors."

"Can I bring Blacky with me?"

For the moment she couldn't think of a good reason why not. "If you feel like carrying him in that case."

Jason fairly leaped out of bed, sending Blacky flying up in the air with a howl. "Great! We're going to have fun!"

Getting up out of a warm bed to go to work on Saturday wasn't Betsy's idea of fun. She headed for the kitchen, where she consumed three cups of black coffee in rapid succession, then pondered the advisability of seeing Nick again.

True to his word, he had not harassed her since the day at the UN. He had barely even spoken to her. He signed up for less and less of her time and rarely stayed late at the office, which was all right with Betsy, because it was a lot easier when she didn't have to see him. She tried not to think about what he was doing with all his free nights. But she had a sneaking suspicion he wasn't staying home reading beneath his flowered sheets. Well, so what? It didn't really concern her, did it?

It took Betsy and Jason working together a good ten minutes before Blacky was successfully put in the carrying case, then Betsy took Jason for a quick breakfast at a Greek coffee shop on Lexington. She ordered bacon and eggs, home fries and toast, and when the check came she was surprised to see that she had consumed it all. And a little of Jason's. It had been awhile since she had even wanted breakfast.

There was nothing redeemable about the weather. After two blocks Jason tired of carrying the case, and Betsy had to take over for him. She noted that Blacky weighed at least twice what he had weighed when she carried him home from Bide-A-Wee, and his howling was proportionately louder.

Jason took one look at the marble-floored lobby of the Cranston Building and said he wished he'd brought his roller skates. She hustled Jason into the elevator and got off at the eighteenth floor. After hanging up their jackets, she led the way down the carpeted hallway to Nick's office.

She was staring at Nick, looking strong and masculine in a sweater almost identical to hers. Jason, once again carrying the case, went right over to Nick.

"Nick, how are you doing? Guess what—I have my cat in this case," rambled Jason.

She noticed that Nick looked a little nonplussed. "Great. Why don't you let him out?"

Jason set the case on top of Nick's desk, then proceeded to do so. An annoyed Blacky leaped out, skidded off the desk, and landed on the floor. He paused to wash his face as Betsy stooped to pick up the papers that had gone along with him.

"His name's Blacky," said Jason. "I wanted to name him Nick, but Mom said no."

Jason could be depended upon for finding the one wrong thing to say in any given situation.

Nick seemed amused. "You want me to show you how to work a word processor, Jason?"

Jason was willing, and after Nick handed her the work he wanted done, Betsy watched as, hand in hand, the two of them set off down the corridor, the cat bounding behind them. She found a machine in the other direction from where they were headed and got to work. The sooner she finished and got out of there the better. She couldn't kid herself that she wasn't still in love with Nick, and being around him was very difficult. She was thankful she had Jason along; he'd at least prevent her from acting foolish.

She was finished and running the job off on the printer when Jason tracked her down.

"Nick's going to take us for a ride to see the ocean. Hurry up, Mom, so we can go."

"We're not going, Jason," she was saying as Nick walked into the room. He stood leaning against the door, his arms folded across his chest.

"Why not? There's nothing else to do. It's a boring weekend, Mom."

He was right—it *was* a boring weekend. With Abby away the four days seemed an eternity to get through. Thanksgiving hadn't been so bad. They had gone to the Macy's parade, and she had cooked a turkey, but since then the time had dragged. Jason had been good, but by today he was starting to get a little stir crazy, and she couldn't blame him.

"We can go to a movie if you want, Jason."

His small face took on its stubborn look. "No. I want to go for a ride with Nick. He's my *friend*, and I never get to see him anymore."

Betsy sighed. "Jason, the cat isn't going to want to go for a ride. Cats hate cars."

"Not Blacky. Blacky will *love* it!"

Betsy looked over at Nick. "I really don't think it was fair of you to ask my son to go for a ride without consulting me first," Betsy said evenly.

Nick looked at Jason, looked back at Betsy, then spread his arms. "He asked me what I was doing today, and I said I was driving out to check on my beach house. He asked if it was on the Atlantic Ocean, I said yes, and he said he'd never seen an ocean, and. . ." His voice trailed off.

Betsy glared down at Jason. "Did you invite yourself along?"

Nick intervened. "No, I invited him. Look, it's a nice drive—I promise to have you back in time for dinner. What's the big deal?"

"Yeah, Mom, what's the big deal?"

"Nick, we've got the cat with us," said Betsy, weakening.

"The cat will love the beach. One big sandbox."

"Yeah, Mom—Blacky will love the beach."

Betsy looked down at Jason. "Where *is* Blacky?"

He shrugged.

"Well, I'm almost finished, so find him and get him in the case."

"Are we going with Nick?"

"Yes," she said, with a weary glance at Nick, "we're going with him."

Any hopes of having Jason ride in the front of the car were shattered when he immediately hopped in the backseat with his cat. Betsy got into the front seat and looked around at the almost new interior of the Cadillac. It seemed much too luxurious for the likes of a small boy and a cat, but that was Nick's problem. He slid in the driver's side, started the engine, then turned on the heater. In a matter of a few blocks the car was toasty warm. Betsy thought of renting the car from Nick to live in until the super did something about their heat.

"Keep Blacky in the case, Jason," warned Betsy.

"But Mom, he wants to look out the window."

"Jason, I have driven with cats before. What they want to do is either sit on the driver's head or under his feet, and either way it could cause an accident. Do *not* let him out until we get there."

"When did you drive with cats?" asked Jason, momentarily diverted.

"We always had cats when I was a kid."

"Oh. Tell me about when you were a kid, Mom."

"Nick isn't interested in hearing about my childhood," she said shortly.

"On the contrary," murmured Nick from beside her.

Betsy turned around to Jason. "When I was a kid we used to go for rides in the country on Sunday, and my brothers and I used to count the cows to see who could get the most. So, Jason, what you can do is count red Volkswagens. If you get to fifty, I'll give you a dollar.''

Jason's eyes instantly went to the windows, where he started keeping a sharp lookout for red VWs.

''Do you always bribe the kid?'' asked Nick.

''That's not bribery, it's creative play,'' she informed him.

''Umm-hmm. My older sister had a similar ruse for me when she wanted to be alone with her boyfriend.''

Betsy glared at him. ''I just thought it would be less distracting for you to drive if he's quiet in the backseat.''

''It's not Jason I find distracting,'' he said in a low voice.

Betsy ignored him and stared straight out the windshield. The only time she had ever been out of Manhattan was coming in from the airport in Queens. They seemed to be beyond that now and on some kind of expressway. An expressway that seemed to be crawling with red VWs, judging by Jason's gleeful tallying.

They drove in silence for about an hour, and Betsy assumed they would be there soon. There wasn't a lot of traffic like there would have been at the beginning of the holiday weekend, and they seemed to be making good time. The car was a pleasure to ride in: roomy, warm, and very smooth handling.

''How much farther is it?'' she finally asked Nick.

''Oh, a ways.''

"Where exactly is it?"

"East Hampton."

"Is that in Queens?"

He chuckled. "No, it's on Long Island."

"It must be nice to have a beach house. Do you use it much?"

"I spend all my weekends out there in the summer. When we split up, Pat took the apartment and I got the beach house."

Betsy wondered if Pat had found herself in Greece yet, but decided it was better not to ask. He might be feeling sentimental about visiting a place he had lived in while married, and talking about her could be upsetting to him.

"Why do you need to go out there today?" she finally asked.

"Oh, I like to check on it a few times during the winter. To see if the boiler's working, that everything's all right. And I had nothing better to do."

Betsy thought if she had Nick's money and his string of women, she would have flown with one down to the Bahamas for the weekend. A little sun would be nice for a change. She pictured herself on a warm beach, wearing just the minimum in a bikini, Nick stretched out beside her. Maybe a couple of exotic drinks sitting beside them. She'd have a golden tan and her hair would be all streaked by the sun. Nick would be dark. His sun-bronzed body would be gleaming, and they'd be so close together on the sand, she'd be able to smell the salt from the ocean on his skin. He'd reach out for her—

Nick was speaking, bringing her out of her reverie

with a jolt. "I asked if you wanted to stop for something to eat."

"Yeah," yelled Jason.

"We just had breakfast," said Betsy.

Nick was already pulling off the highway and into the parking lot of a restaurant. "How about keeping me company, then; I didn't stop to have breakfast."

The cat, over Jason's objections, was left locked in the car. It seemed to be getting even darker out, thought Betsy. And the air had the feel of an impending snowstorm. She heard a noise she couldn't identify, then stopped and listened. "Nick, is that the ocean I hear?"

He nodded. "You'll see it from the window of the restaurant."

So it was the dampness of the water she had felt, not an oncoming storm. Well that was good; she hated driving in snowstorms, even if Nick did seem like an excellent driver.

The restaurant was simple and rather elegant. The wood walls were painted white, the floor was of dark blue tiles. The tables all had linen cloths with silver candleholders in the center. The waitress, in a blue-and-white-checked dress and white apron, lit their candle, then handed them the menus. "Would you like a drink first?" she asked.

Nick looked at Betsy. "I'll have a beer." He ordered her a beer, a Scotch and water for himself, and a Coke for Jason.

"It's been hours since you ate, Betsy—why don't you have something."

Betsy looked at her watch and couldn't believe it

was already three. And they weren't even there yet. "I thought you said you'd have us back by dinner, Nick."

He shrugged. "So you'll have a late dinner. What about you, Jason, you hungry?"

"Starved. Can I have a hamburger? And fries?"

"Whatever you want," Nick said agreeably.

Betsy was also feeling hungry. "I'll have the same as Jason, I guess."

"What about Blacky, Mom? Can I order him something?"

"I'll save him some of my hamburger," Betsy promised.

"Look out the window, Jason, and you'll see the ocean," said Nick.

Betsy went to look, too. She also had never seen an ocean, though she had always considered Lake Michigan just as good as an ocean. There wasn't much to see. The gray of the sky blended with the gray of the ocean, and fog rolling in obscured most of it. *Fog?* She took a closer look. It was snowing out, the snow being blown around in swirls.

She went back to the table. "It's snowing, Nick; I think we ought to turn back."

The waitress was setting their drinks on the table. "The radio says several inches," she informed them. "We might just get snowbound."

"Nick . . ." Betsy was feeling alarmed.

"Betsy, we're almost there. And what's a few inches of snow? I'm sure you've driven in it before, and I've got snow tires on." He sounded reassuring, but she wasn't buying it.

"I'll bet you knew it was going to snow," she accused him.

"Of course I knew; the radio's been saying so all day."

Betsy remembered the radio announcing a "storm front from the west," but at the time it hadn't registered in her mind as snow. Snowbound with Nick. God, it could be one of her fantasies. Except in any romantic daydreams she'd had about him, Jason had never figured as a participant. Nor Blacky.

"How long do we have to be at your house?"

"Not long." His leg moved beneath the table and came to rest alongside hers. She moved hers away and drank some beer. She heard him chuckle. She was glad she was such a constant source of amusement to the man!

Something was nagging at Betsy's memory and she finally realized what it was. "What about the document, Nick?"

He looked perplexed. "What document?"

"The one that you got me to the office to type. The big emergency. You didn't even do anything with it."

"That's right, Betsy. I knew you had a brain behind all that befuddled thinking."

Her eyes widened. "It *wasn't* an emergency. You lied to me."

"Yes, but necessary lies."

Betsy started to get up, and Nick grabbed her wrist. "I want to leave, Nick—right now!"

He released his grip. "It's a long walk, Betsy. And I'm afraid you'll find I'm the only transportation around."

She turned bitter eyes on him. "This is kidnapping!"

He chuckled. "Oh, absolutely. Well planned and well executed."

Jason came back to the table and started chattering to Nick about the ocean and the snow, leaving Betsy helpless to talk. She couldn't let Jason know of the predicament they were in. Not that he'd see it as one; he'd simply view it as an adventure. The unmitigated gall of the man to lure her, through her innocent child, out to his lonely beach house on godforsaken Long Island. She didn't know what he hoped to accomplish by that, but it wasn't going to work. Kidnapped her! She was so furious at the thought, she drank down the rest of her beer to calm herself. And one beer was all she'd better have; she'd have to keep her wits about her. For Jason's sake she was going to have to act calm and dignified. Which meant she couldn't give Nick a disabling kick, grab his car keys, and leave him snowbound all by himself.

She had hardly noticed that the food had arrived. She viewed Nick's thick, juicy steak with lust as she quickly ate her hamburger and fries. She even accepted apple pie for dessert, not knowing when she'd be able to eat again.

"I like a woman with a healthy appetite," murmured Nick, which made Jason immediately commence with a discussion on how much his mother ate. At that moment she felt like kicking them both!

"You didn't leave anything for Blacky, Mom," complained Jason.

"Don't worry, I can feed him at the house," Nick told him.

Betsy's eyes narrowed. "You have food in the house? Since summer?"

He gave her an innocent look. "I had the foresight to stock up yesterday."

"You were there yesterday?"

He smiled. "That's when I got the idea."

"Of all the nefarious—"

"Oh, I agree."

"What's 'nefarious,' Mom?"

"Drop it, Jason!"

In the height of the storm they left the restaurant, driving slowly in very strained silence before they arrived at Nick's house. It was dark out by then, and the snowfall was thick and steady. Jason didn't even ask to see the beach, so Nick led them into a spacious two-story house where, blessedly, there seemed to be plenty of heat. Something else he must have taken care of the day before.

He flicked a switch in the entry hall, which lit several table lamps in the living room, then motioned them inside the room. There was a rough-hewn beamed ceiling, a massive stone fireplace with logs already laid, two large couches covered in beige linen, several easy chairs, and what looked like handmade rag rugs on the polished floorboards. Under different circumstances, Betsy would have fallen in love with it immediately.

Jason was looking around with a frown. "Where's the TV set, Nick?"

"In the den at the back, Jason."

"Can I watch it?"

"Sure."

"Can I let Blacky out?"

"Of course."

"Will you feed him?"

"Jason," said Betsy, "why don't you stay here with us."

Jason looked at Nick and then at his mother. "You two probably want to talk," he said, then left the room.

Nick knelt down by the fireplace and got it lighted. "You have a very astute son," he said. He looked around and saw her still standing in the doorway, a stubborn expression on her face. "You might as well take off your jacket; it's going to be very warm in here soon."

"I think I'll watch television with Jason," she said, turning to go.

He crossed the room quickly and grabbed her by the shoulders, spinning her around. "No, you're not going to watch television. We're going to sit down on that couch, have a drink, and talk together like two civilized adults. Right after I've fed the cat."

Betsy took off her jacket, hung it in the hall closet, then sat down on the couch to wait for the drink she felt she really needed. She could act as civilized and as adult as the next person. And she was *not* going to create a scene with Jason around. She looked around, enjoying the room. There was one whole wall covered with books. Over each couch was a large oil painting of the ocean. And through the French doors, which were now closed and shuttered, she was sure there'd be a view of the ocean.

Nick came into the room, carrying two drinks, and handed one to her. He put a record on the stereo, something classical that she didn't recognize, then he took a seat at the other end of the couch.

He lifted his glass to hers. "To a fruitful discussion," he said, then took a drink.

"I have nothing to discuss," said Betsy, then took a sip of her drink. It tasted like rum, but she didn't know what else was in it. But it was good, and warming, and relaxing.

"Listen, Betsy, I've waited three weeks for you to come to your senses—"

"Three weeks ago is when I *came* to my senses," Betsy cut in.

He gave her a look of extreme patience. "Why don't you try to control yourself while I have my say. Then you may have your turn."

She folded her arms and waited.

"I've done a lot of thinking these past weeks, most of it about us. And not seeing each other just doesn't make any sense."

"It does to me," said Betsy.

"I don't believe that. I've seen you at the office; you don't look any happier than I've looked. I did it your way. I didn't harass you, did I? But it just hasn't worked. It's just plain stupid to break off something that's so good."

"Are you calling me stupid?"

"Yes."

Betsy couldn't for the life of her think of a smart retort.

"I don't know if this matters to you, Betsy, but I haven't been seeing anyone else. I haven't wanted to see anyone else."

Nick? Manhattan's answer to Casanova? She gave him a disbelieving look.

"I'm not lying to you—ask anyone at the office. Ask my secretary. I was getting tired of all that running around, anyway. And you probably won't believe this, either, but most of them were just friends. Including Janine."

Her first impulse was to give him an argument. But she found herself believing him. He was telling her the kinds of things she had longed to hear from him before, so why wasn't she satisfied? He wasn't seeing anyone else, he obviously very much wanted to continue seeing her. And he hadn't given her any ultimatum in the form of a three-month plan. True, he hadn't said he loved her, but it wasn't fair to expect him to fall in love as fast as she had. Maybe he would in time. He damn well *better* in time. She decided it was only stupid stubbornness on her part that was keeping them apart. And she didn't want them to be apart. She didn't even want to be as far apart from him as they were on the couch.

She looked over at him, saw him looking expectant, hopeful, and all of her love for him surged to the surface. She put her drink down on the table, then moved to sit next to him, putting her head against his chest. "I've missed you, Nick."

He put his arm around her shoulders and rested his

head on top of hers. "Thank God I've got a devious mind," breathed Nick. "If I hadn't thought to kidnap you..."

Jason came into the room. "It's warm here, Mom. Can we spend the night?"

Betsy smiled at him. "Yes, we can spend the night."

Jason, not used to getting his way so easily, left the room before she could change her mind.

"Don't you have heat where you live?" Nick asked her.

"It depends on the whims of the super, and I think he's studying to be an Eskimo."

"Why didn't you tell me? I'll send your landlord a letter. Once he sees the law firm letterhead, you'll see some action."

She wondered why she and Abby hadn't thought of that.

He got up from the couch and reached out a hand. "Come on, let's keep Jason company for a while."

"Don't you want to be alone with me?"

He grinned. "I don't trust myself. I think we'd better wait until Jason's in bed."

They watched an old western movie, then Nick told her he had steaks in the refrigerator if they were hungry.

"Let's save them for tomorrow," said Betsy. "I'll go see what else you have."

He seemed to have laid in enough food for a week. Betsy heated up some soup, made toasted cheese sandwiches, then carried it all into the den.

She felt like they were a family as they sat around

eating and watching a hockey game, and she liked the feeling. *Not* that she wanted to get married again, but it would be nice for Jason to have a man around at times.

Finally, when she'd about given up hope of its happening, Jason started to get tired and even asked Nick where he could sleep.

"There's a room upstairs with bunk beds you might like."

"Yeah," said Jason.

"Bunk beds?" questioned Betsy.

"My nephews used to come to visit," Nick told her.

"I don't have any pajamas," said Jason.

"Sleep in your underwear," Betsy told him.

"What are you going to sleep in?"

"I'll wear some of Nick's pajamas," Betsy lied.

Nick turned off the TV, and they took Jason upstairs and put him to bed. Then they went back down to the living room, where the fire was still burning low. Nick turned off a couple of the lamps and sat beside her on the couch.

"Alone at last," he said, grinning.

"You're very good with Jason."

"I like him."

"I'm glad."

"I like his mother even better."

Nick got up and disappeared into the kitchen, returning with a chilled bottle of champagne and two glasses. Betsy hadn't noticed Blacky was in the room with them until the cork popped, making the cat leap sideways, then go chasing after it.

He poured them each some champagne, then proposed a toast. "To an interesting relationship."

"Interesting?"

"With you, Betsy, it will never be boring."

"Nor with you," she concurred.

"Why don't you take off those boots and get comfortable?"

She complied.

"Why don't you sit on my lap?"

She again complied.

And then his mouth was on hers, and all her pent-up longings for him exploded as she returned his hungry kisses. His hand was on her breast as she pressed against him, loving the feel of his hard body against her own.

She noticed the movement but didn't pay any attention to it at first. But then Nick was lifting his head away from hers, and she opened her eyes to see what he was looking at. Blacky had his teeth in Nick's ankle and his claws hanging on to his pants. Nick was shaking his foot, but Blacky hung on tenaciously.

Betsy reached down and swatted the cat, then dislodged each claw from Nick's pants.

"Sorry about that," she murmured, then pulled Nick's head back to her own. She was becoming lost once again in his kisses when she felt him laughing against her mouth. She pulled away and saw that Blacky was now on the back of the couch, his paws playing with Nick's hair.

"What's with that cat?" he asked her.

"He's never seen me with a man before; maybe he's jealous."

"Can you do something with him?"

Betsy slipped the belt out of her pants and looped it over the back of a straight chair, leaving most of it to dangle and tantalize Blacky.

Nick settled himself on the rug in front of the fireplace. "Come on over here—I've always wanted to make love in front of a fire."

Betsy knelt down on the rug beside Nick and leaned over to kiss him. His hands reached up under her sweater to unfasten her bra, and then his fingers squeezed her nipples until they were large and hard. Betsy swayed back and forth as his loving hands aroused her, not in any hurry, wanting the magic moment to be prolonged. He finally pulled her down on top of him, then rolled her over and covered her body with his own.

His hips were moving sensuously against her own, rhythmic, devastating in their ability to excite her. She was pushing hard against him, matching his growing arousal, when Blacky leaped on Nick's back and dug his claws in.

Nick moved off her with a yell of pain, then noted Betsy's expression.

"Go on, laugh. As though Jason weren't enough protection, you had to get a cat, too. A guard cat."

Betsy burst out laughing. She couldn't believe that such a large man could be felled by such a small cat.

He reached out a hand and helped her up from the floor. "Come on."

"Where are we going?"

"To the bedroom. It has a door."

She smiled up at him. "Good, I think I'm getting

too old for making love on the floor, anyway. Give me a comfortable mattress anytime.''

"My sentiments exactly." Nick grinned.

Making sure Blacky was locked outside the bedroom, Nick turned on one bedside lamp, then reached for Betsy. But she shook her head and slowly began to undress. Nick did the same, and they watched each other as each garment was dropped to the floor. When they were both naked he picked her up and carried her to the bed.

"Now, if there are no more interruptions. . ."

"Can you lock the bedroom door?" Betsy asked.

"Do you want me to?"

She nodded.

"At least I'm not doped up this time," he said.

"I'm glad to hear it," teased Betsy.

"Do you want me to bring the champagne up?"

"No."

"Is there anything you want before I begin?"

She shook her head. "You're all I want," she told him.

"I hope you mean that," he said, then got on the bed and drew her to him. He made love to her as though they had all the time in the world. He kissed her deeply, his tongue exploring her mouth. She moved one of her smooth legs on top of his, liking the feel of his scratchy hair against her. She moved one hand across his chest, memorizing its surface as he pulled her even closer to him.

"You're so beautiful," he said, his voice a soft moan as he buried his face against the soft curve of her throat, his moving lips a sensuous flutter that didn't cease until they reached one warm breast. She gasped as his tongue played gently with her taut nipple, and she closed her eyes, feeling something inside her open like the petals of a flower brought to life by the warmth of the sun.

It wasn't only his mouth, but his strong, hard body against her, that aroused her softness into willing response. Her hands moved over him, traveling across the muscled expanse of his chest and stomach.

He rolled her over on her back and looked down at her. Her eyes were held by the beauty of his male nakedness, the graceful symmetry of muscles and taut flesh. He moved on top of her, his skin hot against her fingertips, making her shiver with its velvety hardness.

Their eyes held as his hard flesh claimed her, the two merging into one. Over and over she cried out his name, made more on fire by his hands, mouth, and thrusting body than she had ever been before. His gentle hands molded her hips, moving with them as she responded willingly beneath him.

In tune to each other's every move, as though they had been together a thousand times before, they climbed the heights of ecstasy and, when they could go no farther, exploded violently together in a moment of such awesome proportions Betsy thought she was going to lose consciousness. He held on to her tightly as she clung to him, and she knew she felt a greater love for him than she'd ever be able to express.

They stayed that way long moments until the rocking world once more settled in its orbit, then he moved off her and cradled her in his arms.

"Does your one-time-only policy mean just one time per night?" asked Nick, a gleam in his eyes.

"Certainly not," said Betsy.

"Insatiable nut!"

Betsy had never been called insatiable before. She liked the sound of it. "Well, they say a woman's sex drive increases as she gets older," said Betsy, "just as a man's decreases." She gave him a wicked smile.

"I'll show you just how mine's decreasing," threatened Nick.

"Please do," she said archly.

He grinned at her. "Have you ever made love in the shower?"

She shook her head. "I've never made love on the beach or in the snow, either. Are we going to do that, too?"

He laughed. "With you it would probably be fun." He got out of bed and dragged her after him. "Come on, I'm covered with sweat, and I want to see how you are underwater."

Betsy was glad to see there was a shower stall and not a tub. Nick turned on the water, adjusted the temperature, and then they stepped inside. They soaped each other's bodies gently at first, then with growing enthusiasm. They both were fully aroused by the time he pulled her to him, and after some artful maneuverings, they were making love with the warm water beating down on them. She was so shaken when they were finished, she had to cling to him for support.

When she was standing in a happy daze while he toweled her dry, he said, "Now do you know what we're going to do?"

She looked at him in amazement. "What are you, Superman?"

He laughed. "No. I wish I were, but I'm not. What I was going to suggest was that I go downstairs, bring up the rest of the champagne...and maybe some pretzels...and we can watch a late movie in bed. One of my favorites is on—*Casablanca*. What do you say?"

She nodded happily. "It sounds perfect. I love old romantic movies."

He gave her a wicked look. "I love old romantic women."

He moved quickly before she could hit him on the rear end with the towel. "Get in bed, shweetheart. I'll be right back."

"That was a lousy Bogart," she yelled after him.

Halfway through the movie Nick proved that he might be Superman after all.

BETSY WOKE UP with the feeling that something was different. Not only was she happy, she was also warm. And, if she wasn't mistaken... She looked next to her. Yes, there was a warm body beside her. The memories of the night before came flooding back. He was sleeping on his side, his back turned to her. She got up on one elbow to look down at his sleeping face. He looked so sweet when he was sleeping, so appealing. She wondered what he would do if she rolled him over and woke him up by...

Faintly, in the distance, she could hear Jason calling Blacky. She'd better get up before he found her and Nick, instead.

She gave Nick one last look of longing, then got quietly out of bed. Oh, well—poor Superman probably deserves a rest.

She went into the connecting bathroom and washed her face, wishing she had a toothbrush with her. Then she dressed in her cords and sweater and went downstairs to find Jason. He was in the kitchen, trying to find cat food and getting frustrated in his efforts.

"There's nothing for Blacky to eat, Mom."

"I'll find him something, but he'd better go out first."

"Out? In the snow?"

Betsy nodded, not wanting to think about what the cat had used for a box during the night.

"But Blacky never goes out."

"He does this morning." Betsy opened the back door and looked out on several inches of snow. The sun was out, the sky was blue, and it was incredibly cold.

Blacky wouldn't go near the door, and Betsy finally picked up the skittish cat and set him outside. He stood there trembling in rage for a minute, then slowly started digging his paws in the snow. She closed the door to give him some privacy.

The kitchen was large and well equipped, and Betsy found it a pleasure to work in after the dollhouse-size one in her apartment. She had coffee on to boil, ham and eggs frying, and Jason fixing toast when Nick came in to the kitchen, wearing sweat pants and a navy blue sweater and looking his usual sexy self. He came over to the stove, where she stood, and hugged her from behind. She leaned back into him, the picture of contentment.

"You can let Blacky in now, Jason," she said, then gave Nick a quick kiss while Jason was opening the door.

A lot of cold air came in with the disgruntled cat, who was not too disgruntled to want to share their ham and eggs, though, she noticed.

Nick got out plates and silverware and set the round maple table in front of the window, and Betsy brought the food to the table. There wasn't much talking while they consumed the food with good appetites, but afterward, when Nick and Betsy were having second cups of coffee, Jason mentioned for about the third time how much he liked the house and how neat it was that it was right on the beach.

"You'll like it even better in the summer," Nick told him. "We can all play football in the sand."

Betsy looked at Nick as the words sank in. At that moment she was happier to hear them than she would have been to hear his declaration of love. If he was thinking in terms of their being together next summer, then she was certainly not in his three-month category of women.

He had been saying something to her, but she hadn't heard it.

"I was asking you if you're still playing football on Saturdays," he repeated.

"Oh, it got too cold. Hardly anyone was showing up anymore, so we finally just dropped it."

"Hey, Nick—let's go out and play some football now," said Jason.

Nick shook his head. "I think it's too cold out for football, Jason. We can find something to do in here."

"No, it isn't, Nick—I never get sick."

Nick looked at Betsy for support.

"Jason, Nick gets colds very easily," said Betsy.

His look of support changed to a look of annoyance.

Jason looked at him with concern. "You should drink lots of orange juice, Nick, that's what I do."

"I *don't* get colds that easily," muttered Nick. "Do you play chess, Jason?"

Betsy stared after Jason as he followed Nick from the table. He might think he played chess, but she knew differently. He played it exactly like checkers, which Nick was soon to find out.

She was a little incensed that they had just walked out and left her to do the dishes. Obviously his wife had spoiled him thoroughly. Not that Tom had ever helped, but she and Nick weren't even married.

She was mentally composing a speech on women's lib to direct to him when he stuck his head in the kitchen and said, "Leave the dishes. I'll do them later."

She was about to do just that when she noticed the dishwasher built in to the cupboards and decided the whole thing wasn't that important. She shoved the dishes in, turned it on, then went to join them in the den. As she suspected, they were playing checkers with the chess set.

She sat down on the couch next to Nick and watched him beat Jason rather quickly.

"What do you usually do on Sundays?" Nick asked her.

"Oh, read *The Times*."

"Me, too. Why don't I drive into town and pick up a couple?"

"A *couple*?"

"Yeah, so we can each have our own crossword puzzle."

"One's enough," Betsy said dryly.

He was back in fifteen minutes with the paper, and some comic books for a delighted Jason. Betsy took the sports section to see what football games were being televised that day, and watched surreptitiously as Nick finished the crossword puzzle in under twenty minutes. She mentally revised her list of what they had in common.

"The Giants are playing the Bears, Nick. Is it okay if I put it on?" she asked him.

He looked up from the financial section, one part of the paper she never even glanced at. "Who are the Jets playing?"

She looked it up. "San Diego."

"Let's watch that," he said in a rather peremptory fashion.

She was silent for a moment. "Do you have two sets?"

He looked at her over the paper. "What for?"

"I want to watch the Bears and the Giants."

"Why?" His tone was incredulous. "Neither of them has won a game all season."

"One of them will have after today," she pointed out.

He put down the paper. "Betsy, I find it hard to believe that someone as knowledgeable about football as yourself would rather watch a couple of second-rate teams than two contenders."

"I happen to have some loyalty, Nick; I'm a Bears fan."

He shook his head in disgust. "There's another set in the guest room, where Jason slept."

She checked what channel it was on, then got up.

His voice stopped her. "You'd really rather watch that game all by yourself than sit down here with me and watch the Jets?"

"I could say the same thing to you."

Jason looked up from his comic book. "Are you two fighting?"

"Your mother and I spend a good deal of time fighting," Nick said to Jason.

"Mostly, Jason, because Nick is a very stubborn man."

"*I'm* stubborn?"

Betsy walked out of the room and went upstairs to find the other TV set. It was a small portable, and she carried it back downstairs and into the den, setting it up beside the large one. While Nick watched in amazement she tuned both sets in to separate games, leaving the sound off on both.

"Very good, Betsy, but what if I want to hear what's going on?"

She gave him a smile of sweetness. "Anyone as knowledgeable about football as you, Nick, shouldn't *need* the sound to know what's going on."

"Want to play a game of chess while we watch?" asked Nick, a competitive gleam in his eyes.

"Sure," she said, resetting the chessboard with one eye on the TV.

Betsy wasn't a very good player. She didn't play it like checkers, exactly, but she liked to play fast and never gave much thought to her moves. People who played like Nick, thinking every move out carefully and taking forever, drove her crazy. She barely even paid any attention to what she was doing, being more interested in the football game. But by pure luck, and a series of moves so random, they seemed to drive Nick berserk wondering just what her strategy was, she won the game. She was just as surprised as he but kept her face impassive and acted as though she had known exactly what she was doing and that the win was expected.

He was staring at the board, trying to figure out where he went wrong. He kept recalling moves of hers out loud, questioning her about them, but she couldn't even remember what she had done, so she told him to be quiet so she could watch the game.

He started to set up the chessboard again. "Let's try another," he said to her.

"It was kind of boring, Nick; I'd rather just watch the football game," she said casually.

"*Boring?* I've never been told I play a boring game before," said Nick.

She got up from the floor and sat beside him on the

couch, leaning against him and nuzzling her face against his shoulder. "I can't concentrate on both at the same time," she told him, which was true, but she knew he wouldn't believe her.

The Bears won, but Betsy made a point of not gloating. The Jets lost, and Betsy was afraid Nick was going to put his foot through the TV screen. He didn't, though; just slammed out to the kitchen and made them all steak sandwiches. Afterward, they decided they had better head back to the city. The holiday traffic would be bad, and the roads were icy.

Jason quickly fell asleep in the backseat, Blacky howled intermittently, and Betsy snuggled up beside Nick and distracted him from his driving.

"You owe me a rematch on that game, you know," he said to her as they approached Manhattan.

"Anytime, Nick," she said, sounding as though it would be mere child's play for her.

"Listen, Betsy—you're not going to find some excuse to get rid of me again, are you?"

She kissed him on the side of his neck. "Would I do that?"

His arm went around her. "I don't know; I still can't figure you out."

"I promise I won't unless I have a very good reason," she said.

"Does this mean we can date now?"

She was silent for a moment. "I think we're doing all right without dating, don't you?"

"What do I have to do, make up some emergency to get you down to the office every time I want to see you?"

"You've been pretty good at it so far."

He chuckled. "I have, haven't I? We lawyers are a devious lot. Seriously, though, I'd like to take you places."

"I don't mind going places with you."

"You just don't want to call it dating, huh?"

She nodded in agreement.

When he pulled up in front of her building he gave her a long, slow kiss before waking Jason. "Thanks again for helping me out in an emergency, Betsy," he told her as she and Jason were getting out of the car. She was still laughing when she let herself into the apartment.

Chapter Eight

"I really know I'm getting old, Abby, when I can't get through chapter three of a children's book," said Betsy in disgust, setting the book down on the table and helping herself to her second doughnut.

Abby picked it up and read the title. *"Beginning Chess—Ages 8-12.* Why do you have to learn chess?"

"Because I beat Nick in a fluke game, and he keeps bugging me to play him again."

"How have you gotten out of it so far?"

Betsy grinned. "By casting glances of longing toward his bedroom at the crucial moment. But one of these times that's not going to work."

Abby shrugged. "So tell him it was a fluke and that you really don't know how to play."

Betsy's eyes widened. "No way—I want to beat him again. Maybe I could take lessons somewhere."

Abby was looking askance. "You're really competitive, aren't you?"

"You'd be too if you grew up with several older brothers who always beat you at everything. Anyway, I enjoy it; I think Nick does, too."

"I'd say you two are perfectly matched," observed Abby.

Betsy sank back in her chair with a smile. "I think

so, too. Now if only that man would tell me he loves me, everything would be perfect.''

"No, it wouldn't. Next you'd be wanting him to swear he'll love you forever, then you'd be wanting him to propose. . . anyway, have you told him?''

"That I love him?''

Abby nodded.

"No.'' She sounded surprised at the question.

"Then what's the big deal?''

Betsy leaned across the table. "The big deal is, I think he should tell me first. He's the man.''

Abby shook her head. "I don't know, Betts, it doesn't sound like you've come a long way, baby, if you know what I mean.''

"Abby, I'd feel really stupid if I told him I loved him and then there was this long silence. If *you* know what *I* mean.''

"I think all it means is that you two are competitive in everything, even revealing your feelings.''

Betsy took another doughnut and broke off a piece to dunk in her coffee. "I'll tell you, it's very difficult not saying it to him. One of these times, in the heat of the moment, I'm afraid I'm going to blurt it out.''

"And when you do, he'll probably reciprocate. Anyway, anyone can see he's head over heels about you. He calls you all the time, he takes you everywhere—he even got us heat in the building.''

"Thank God,'' breathed Betsy.

"Yeah, I think the temperature is supposed to soar to ten degrees today.''

"There's no talk at the office, is there?'' Betsy asked.

"Are you kidding? The whole office is buzzing."

"About *us*?" Betsy asked worriedly. She hated the thought of being the center of office gossip.

"No, just about Nick. He doesn't flirt anymore; he doesn't date anyone from the office, or so they think; women seldom call him anymore, and when they do his secretary tells them he's in conference. He's a changed man, and all because of you."

"I'm glad the office doesn't know," said Betsy, "although I think Lisa and Christine suspect."

"How are you going to keep it quiet at the Christmas party? Nick's pretty demonstrative, as if you didn't know."

"I wasn't planning on going."

"You've got to—it'll be great. You've never seen food until you see the spread they spring for. *And* an open bar. *And* live music."

"Well, we can't both go, Abby; it's not worth getting a baby-sitter for."

"That's where you're wrong—it's worth it, all right, but we don't have to. I figure I'll go directly from work and stay from six to nine, then I'll come home, and you can go for the rest of it. And don't worry, there'll still be plenty of food."

Carla came out of the bathroom, still dressed in her pajamas, a thick coating of talcum powder covering her face. She walked slowly over to her mother, her eyes drooping, and said in a soft, pained voice, "I don't feel well, Mother. Can I stay home sick today?"

"Don't you have an arithmetic test today?" Abby asked her.

Carla nodded. "I feel terrible about missing it."

Betsy was biting her lip to keep from laughing.

"What's the matter with you?" asked Abby, one brow lifted sardonically.

Carla first put her hands to her stomach, then moved them to her chest. "I don't know, I feel bad all over." She paused and looked up at her mother. "Don't I seem awfully pale to you?"

Tongue in cheek, Abby nodded. "Oh, yes, you look pale, all right, and I'll bet the bathroom floor is covered with talcum powder."

Carla's eyes narrowed in defiance. "I'm *really* sick. I might even be dying."

Betsy's eyes were dancing as they looked over at Abby. "I don't mind if she stays home today. We can watch soap operas together and drink lots of hot tea."

Carla's lower lip drooped. "Soap operas? I *hate* soap operas."

"There's nothing much else to do when you're sick in bed," said Abby.

The thought of an entire day of watching soaps with Betsy seemed to inspire a miraculous recovery. Carla decided she felt much better and went back to the bathroom to get ready for school.

Betsy was laughing. "I can remember trying that exact same thing on *my* mother, talcum powder and all. Only *I* got away with it."

"Mothers are smarter these days," mused Abby.

Jason came in and grabbed the last doughnut. "Is Nick picking me up tonight?" he asked.

Betsy nodded. "Tuesdays and Thursdays, you should know that by now."

Nick, with Betsy's permission, was teaching Jason how to play handball at his athletic club two evenings a week. Those times were the highlight of Jason's week, and from what Nick told her, the boy was far better at handball than he was at chess.

"That's another indication of what we were talking about before," said Abby.

Betsy looked at her questioningly.

"He's even acting like a you-know-what to Jason."

"What's a you-know-what?" asked Jason.

"Never mind," said Betsy.

THE CHRISTMAS PARTY was being held the week before Christmas, and while Betsy did her Christmas shopping, she kept her eyes open for something to wear to it. Abby had told her the women got quite dressed up, but even before that Betsy had decided to get a dress. She realized that no one at the office, including Nick, had ever seen her in anything but drab office clothes or pants, and for the party she wanted to look different.

Betsy found New York beautiful at Christmastime, with the exquisitely decorated store windows that people queued up to see and the insides decorated just as beautifully, with piped Christmas music or strolling carollers. But the crowds of people almost drove her crazy. She loved Macy's normally, but now it was like trying to get on a subway during rush hour to even enter the store, and once inside there were long lines at every cash register.

She had thought long and hard about a present for

Nick. Clothes seemed like such a boring choice, and jewelry seemed too personal. It was when she was buying Jason a computer football game that she spied the computer chess sets. The salesman had time at the moment to show her the different models. The one she chose was a lot of money, but she figured if it got him off the subject of *her* playing, it was well worth the price. She and Jason were spending Christmas with him at his beach house, and she wanted them both to have toys to play with on Christmas morning. It was her experience that men always reverted to children at Christmastime.

She also purchased three colorful felt stockings for them to hang up on Christmas Eve. She didn't think she'd put presents in them, just lots of Christmas candy and fruit. She also bought a down vest for Jason to give his father for Christmas. The day after Christmas Jason would be flying to Chicago, where Tom would meet him at the airport, and then they'd fly out to Colorado.

Nick *had* been wonderful with Jason. It wasn't like what Abby thought, though; he treated him more like a friend than a son. And Betsy didn't think there was any comparing going on in Jason's mind between his father and Nick. Tom had always been an attentive father and given Jason a lot of his time. She was afraid, knowing Jason's big mouth, that Tom would hear a lot about Nick during the ski trip, but that couldn't be avoided.

In a way, now, Betsy was glad Jason was going away for a week. She'd miss him, but she'd also be able to spend an entire weekend alone with Nick.

When she saw him now she'd often stay late at his apartment, but never the entire night. She felt it was her place to be there when Jason got up in the morning. But now she had Christmas weekend and New Year's weekend to look forward to, and she was every bit as excited about the upcoming holidays as the children were.

After looking unsuccessfully in Macy's and Altman's and all the small shops in between, she had almost given up hope of finding the perfect dress. She had walked up Fifth Avenue to see the window displays at Lord & Taylor that Abby had told her about. Each window was a separate scene set in Victorian times and each more exquisite than the last. She had never been in Lord & Taylor and decided to go inside and look around. Unlike Macy's, it wasn't frantic, so she took the escalator up to the different floors to see what she could find. She tried on several dresses before she spotted the perfect outfit. The jacket and skirt were of patchwork in different patterns of satin and velvet. The velvet patches were predominantly deep burgundy and emerald green; the satin were antique ivory. The top was of ivory satin with thin spaghetti straps and a low, draped neck. Despite the fact that she was wearing running shoes when she tried it on, and thus lost some of the overall effect, she knew it was perfect. It was New York sophisticated combined with an old-world charm. She was lucky enough to find some burgundy suede high heels to go with it, and she decided she'd borrow Abby's white fake-fur coat with the hood to wear over the top.

In the lingerie department she found what she had been looking for for Abby: a red velour bathrobe to take the place of her raggedy flannel one. She decided to visit the children's department, too. If she could find something for Carla, her shopping would be finished.

When she finally saw it, it was so perfect for Carla, she didn't care that it was more than she had wanted to spend. It was a plastic hat box. Opened, it revealed a mirror in the top and three Dynel wigs in a child's size. One was long and straight and platinum blond, one was shoulder-length in red, and the third was a short black Afro. She could just see the child's expression when she tried them on.

When it came to Christmas presents the biggest difficulty proved to be Blacky. On three different occasions she picked up a catnip mouse for him while she was out shopping. She'd take it home, hide it in a drawer or cupboard, and within hours the cat would have managed to find it, and she would find the poor mouse torn to bits all over the floor. The cat, a dazed look in his eyes, would be walking around the room on wobbly legs. She finally bought one last mouse and decided to keep it in the bottom of her purse. She would just have to carry it around with her until Christmas morning.

On the evening of the office Christmas party Betsy spent a lot of time on her appearance. Just once she would like to really dazzle Nick, she decided. She had blown dry her hair, straightening out the curls until her hair swept up and away from her face in gentle waves, a more sophisticated look than she generally achieved. Darkening her eyebrows slightly and her lashes a lot, she put on some soft brown eyeshadow that brought out the green in her eyes. She used some liquid gold rub to highlight her cheekbones and the top of her nose, giving the effect of her having been out in the sun, then put on a wet-looking red lip gloss. She fastened emerald studs in her earlobes—an anniversary gift from Tom one year—and a matching emerald dinner ring. When she had dressed in her new outfit she surveyed herself in the mirror and thought she had never looked better. If she had wanted to attract Nick's attention, this would be exactly how she would want to look. Since she already had his attention, she was hoping he'd take one look at her and fall madly in love. Abby arrived home from the party looking as pretty as a Christmas tree ornament in her glittery silver jump suit and matching boots. She took one look at Betsy, let out a low whistle, and said, "You're going to stun that office when you make your entrance, kid. And I think Nick's going to find he has a lot of competition." She handed her white furry coat to Betsy and helped her on with it.

"I don't even know where the party is, Abby."

"The Time-Life Building near Rockefeller Center. Just tell the cabby, he'll know where it is. And don't worry about being late—live it up."

It was cold out and rather damp. Betsy put the hood of the coat up so her hair wouldn't curl from the moisture. She found a taxi right away and was at the building in ten minutes. She took the elevator up to the banquet rooms the office had rented for the night and checked her coat before following the sound of the music to a noisy, crowded room. There were two Christmas trees, a group playing in one corner, and a lot of festive-looking people.

The night staff surrounded her immediately, all of them complimenting her on her appearance, and George even asked her to dance. But Betsy's eyes were caught by the awesome display of food spread out on long tables.

"Later, George," she murmured as she took a plate and began heaping it with food.

"Somehow I knew you'd head for the food first," said Nick, by her side.

She gave him a sidelong glance. "I'm sure you didn't neglect it."

"On the contrary, I've been waiting for you. Although I don't think I could have held out much longer," he admitted.

She gave him an admiring look. "I wouldn't have been able to hold out for ten minutes."

"Some of us have more willpower than others, that's all. Now, let's find ourselves a quiet little table—"

"Nick, I can't eat with you—people will talk."

"They're talking already."

"Yes, but they don't know what they're talking about."

He chuckled. "Oh, I think they know *exactly* what they're talking about."

Betsy looked at him in consternation. He was one of the partners, and she was only a night staff secretary; she was afraid some of the other partners might disapprove. "Please, let me sit with the night workers while I eat. Go dance with someone and throw off suspicion."

"I've already been doing that for a couple of hours."

It would have been all right if he had done it at her suggestion, but she hated the thought of him doing it on his own. And I never thought I was the jealous type, she mused.

She saw Christine and George at one of the tables and went over to join them. She began to eat, all the while listening to the steady stream of gossip George was imparting to Christine. Christine finally broke in and addressed Betsy. "You look absolutely elegant, Betsy—and I love what you've done to your hair."

At least *someone* noticed, thought Betsy, her mouth too full to do anything but smile her thanks at Christine. She had generous portions of prime rib, and baked trout, and duck, helpings of mashed potatoes and candied yams, several fresh vegetables, four different salads, and a mound of pâté to spread on her hot rolls. She only hoped she'd have room left for some of the delicious desserts she fully intended to go up for.

She saw Nick seated at the next table, and he lifted his fork and nodded to her when their eyes met. He was looking devastatingly attractive in black slacks, a black tweed sport jacket, and a white silk shirt. She started thinking about how she found him even more attractive without his clothes, then felt herself blushing.

It took her the better part of an hour to consume

all the food that appealed to her. She decided to defer dessert for a while, and instead went over to the bar and asked for a glass of red wine. Several of the lawyers who had never spoken to her before came by while she was standing there and asked her if she was enjoying the party. She told them she was enjoying it far too much and would have to do a lot of dancing to compensate for all the food she had eaten. Three immediately asked her to dance, which rather flustered Betsy. She wondered if she had been flirting. She saw Nick on the dance floor with one of the paralegals, so she took the hand of the first one who had asked and followed him out onto the floor.

The group was playing a fast tune with a disco beat. Betsy hadn't danced in years, but the wine gave her the confidence she might normally have lacked. She noticed the theater people were all dancing like professionals, and even Nick looked pretty good on the floor. She moved in time to the music, conscious that she hadn't worn a pair of high heels in a long time and hoping she wouldn't turn an ankle and look like a fool.

When the song ended and the group swung into a slower number, Nick came over and asked her to dance. He pulled her in close to him, his head resting on hers. She was about to pull away when she saw that other couples were dancing just as close, some even closer. She squeezed his hand and put her head on his shoulder, loving the feel of his strong legs guiding hers around the dance floor.

"You look different tonight. What did you do to your hair?" he murmured in her ear.

That's all he could say? That she looked *different*? "I straightened it with my hair dryer," she said shortly.

"If you had worn that outfit to work, I would have seduced you then and there," he said.

Well, that was a little better. She felt herself melting against him. "I don't think we should dance together more than once," she told him.

"The way you look tonight, Betsy, I'd dance with you more than once if you were a total stranger."

It wasn't just that the others might talk. Being this close to Nick, even in a crowded room, was doing the same things to her it always did, only then they were usually alone. She could feel her nipples harden beneath the thin satin top as they pressed against his chest, and a familiar warmth was enveloping her body. "Well, not more than twice, then," she said a little breathlessly.

"Hell, I've danced with Christine more than that already."

She stiffened a moment, then relaxed. "Are you trying to make me jealous?"

He chuckled. "Maybe."

"It won't work. I happen to know she's seeing a director at the moment and it's pretty serious."

"What about us, Betsy, are we pretty serious?"

She was silent for a moment. "I don't know, Nick, are we?"

He danced her over to a corner of the floor, turned his back on the other dancers, then bent down to kiss her. The feel of his hard mouth against hers ignited her, causing her to cling to him helplessly. At that moment she didn't care who might see them together.

One hand moved up her breast over the thin fabric. "Let's get out of here."

She was trembling as she looked up at him. "We couldn't do that."

"Sure we could. Go get your coat and walk out. I'll meet you down in the lobby in five minutes." His hand dropped and he took her by the shoulders and turned her around. "Go on—hurry up, or I won't be able to guarantee to continue my good behavior."

She looked over her shoulder at him. "Is that a promise?"

He shook his head. "You're as bad as I am, do you know that?"

She knew it and had trouble understanding it. She had never been that way with Tom. She and Nick seemed to be perfectly attuned sexually, and the only problem was that they wanted each other all the time. The week before, he had taken her to a French movie. Ten minutes into the film, as the French lovers frolicked on the screen, they took one look at each other and left quickly, almost running back to Nick's apartment. Now the party. She had been looking forward to dancing with Nick, but dancing just wasn't enough. She wanted to be held in his arms where there weren't dozens of eyes assessing their every move. Well, the party really didn't mean anything to her compared to being alone with him. The dress, the time she spent on her appearance, all of it had been only for his benefit, no one else.

She nodded, her eyes shining. She looked around

to see if anyone was watching. No one appeared to be, so she went to get her coat, then took the elevator downstairs.

Nick met her in less than a minute, looking handsome in a tweed overcoat with a velvet collar that she had never seen before. He took her hand, and they went outside into a softly falling snow. He was about to hail a taxi when she stopped him.

"Could we walk over to Rockefeller Center? I've never seen the tree."

He looked down at her feet. "Can you walk in those?"

"I can try," she said wryly, thinking if she could dance in them, she could probably walk. And it was only a block away.

The first view of the tree took her breath away. Leading up to it were gigantic white angels, looking as though they were made of spun glass. The tree itself was spectacular: enormous, with multicolored balls the size of basketballs. Spread out below it were the ice skaters, some of them performing like professionals.

Nick had his arm around her while they watched the skaters. He started to lift the hood over her wet head, then said, "Now you're looking back to normal."

She gave him a questioning look.

"Your hair—the snow's making it curl up."

She should have known it wouldn't last. She put her arms around his waist and hugged him, her head against his chest. "Let's go over to your place," she said softly.

He raised a brow. "Are you propositioning me, Ms. Miller? I must say that kind of conduct is frowned upon at office Christmas parties."

"I'm sure it happens to you at every Christmas party, Mr. Creme," she murmured, causing him to laugh out loud.

Hand in hand they went back out to Fifth Avenue. The gothic spires of St. Patrick's Cathedral looked magnificent lit up in the snow, and on the steps of the church a group of young people were singing Christmas carols. There wasn't a taxi in sight, so they joined the singers for a few songs, then started east on Fifty-fourth Street. They were halfway to Nick's apartment by the time they caught a cab. It was warm inside, and the garrulous driver tried to carry on a conversation with them. He was out of luck; Nick and Betsy were too busy kissing.

Riding up to his floor, Nick opened her coat and put his arms around her. "Ever made love in an elevator?" he whispered in her ear.

"No, but I'd love to," she teased, a look of mischief in her eyes. She reached out to unbuckle his belt, and he moved back out of her reach, a look of mock horror in his eyes.

"Really, Ms. Miller—you forget yourself!"

"I'm not forgetting anything at all, Mr. Creme." She grinned.

Once in the apartment, he hung up their coats, then turned on the stereo to some soft Bartok and poured them each a brandy. They were both so eager to make love, it almost seemed necessary to prolong the moment.

She took a sip of the warming brandy, then leaned against him and began to loosen his tie. Her breathing had quickened and she felt flutters of anticipation in her stomach.

"When you walked into that party, looking like something off the cover of *Vogue*, only a whole lot sexier, I wanted to shout to the world that you belonged to me," he said, his lips in her hair.

"I don't belong to you," she said, removing his tie and starting on the top button of his shirt.

"Like hell you don't," he growled.

She undid his shirt, pulled it out of his pants, then pushed up his undershirt so that she could nuzzle his chest with her nose. She was fairly floating in happiness at his words. She wanted to belong to him; she wanted to belong to him forever.

He took the glass out of her hand and set it down on a table. Then he helped her off with her jacket. "I wanted you on the dance floor, Betsy, do you know that?"

Her hands were now successfully unbuckling his belt. "I wanted you too, Nick. I practically always want you."

"*Practically* always?"

"Well, I don't necessarily dwell on it when I'm eating my Frosted Flakes in the morning."

He pushed her thin straps off her shoulders, and they slid down her arms. The loose top fell to her waist, revealing her braless breasts.

"Shameless hussy. Coming to the Christmas party without underwear."

If there had been a bra in that entire crowd, Betsy

would have been surprised. "I wanted to excite you," she said softly.

"You excite me no matter what you're wearing. Or not wearing."

She undid his pants, and they fell to the floor. She reached around and unzipped her skirt and let it drop, leaving her clad only in panty hose, shoes, and black lace bikinis.

Nick's eyes were devouring her. "If I were a fetishist, I'd tell you to leave them on," he said, "but since I'm not. . ." He slid his hands slowly inside her panty hose and slid them and her panties down her legs. She kicked off her shoes, and then she was naked, pressed close against him. They kissed deeply, urgently, and then they were sinking down onto the soft rug.

"I've got clean sheets on the bed," he said, already covering her body with his own.

"The bedroom's much too far away," murmured Betsy.

They made love quickly, urgently, their bodies fitting together like two connecting parts of a puzzle. The chemistry between them was explosive, bringing Betsy to heights of feeling unknown to her during her marriage. She had only read of such things, never experienced them before. And the experience was mind-shattering.

She clung to him afterward, not wanting to let him go. "You have no idea what you do to me," she breathed shakily.

"I have a very good idea. You do the same to me."

She shook her head. "No, it's different. I've read about such things in women's magazines before, but

I always thought it was all just propaganda; I never thought it would really happen to me.''

"Don't think I'm the same with everyone, Betsy; you inspire me. With you I'm like a kid again. Oh, a little more subtle, but just as energetic. Believe me, my marriage wasn't like this, either.''

Ours would be perfect, she thought to herself, wishing he would say the words. Instead, he was getting up and lighting a cigarette, then finishing off his brandy. "You hungry?" he asked her.

"Good heavens, no—I stuffed myself at the party.''

"You're usually hungry afterward.''

"Maybe later.'' She smiled.

They went into the bedroom and made love again, slowly this time, their hands and mouths exploring each other's bodies. This time it was gentle and unhurried, his eyes smiling down into hers, telling her what his lips refused to say, and she answered with her own eyes, the love she felt for him shining out of their depths.

He made her a cup of coffee before she left. She hated having always to get up, get dressed, and go home. Which was one point in favor of marriage, she guessed—never having to get up and go home. In the dark. And in the cold.

Chapter Nine

Christmas was on a Sunday. The office closed down at noon on Friday, and Betsy and Abby planned on spending Friday night together, decorating their trees and exchanging presents. Saturday, Abby and Carla would leave to spend Christmas with Abby's parents in New Jersey, and Nick would be picking up Betsy and Jason and the cat to drive out to Long Island.

They had both bought small trees on Third Avenue. Betsy had decorated hers inexpensively with white lights and a profusion of candy canes and red bows. She reasoned that expensive ornaments would probably be destroyed by Blacky anyway. Abby, however, had a collection of horses she used on her tree: little wooden rocking horses, miniature hobbyhorses, satin horses made in China, and there were even a few unicorns interspersed among the horses. Betsy thought it the most charmingly decorated tree she had ever seen and vowed to start collecting horse ornaments herself after Christmas, when they went on sale.

The childrens' choice for dinner was pizza, so they ordered two large ones with everything on them and had them delivered.

"What did you get Nick for Christmas?" asked Abby, picking the anchovies off her piece.

Betsy picked up the anchovies and added them to hers. "Are you ready for this?" She looked around to make sure Jason wasn't listening, as he'd be sure to tell Nick. "A computer chess set."

Abby's eyes sparkled. "Absolutely brilliant. I wonder what he's getting you?"

Betsy wondered, too. There wasn't one single thing she really wanted or needed, and she couldn't fathom what Nick's taste in presents would be. Just so he didn't get *her* a computer chess set. "I haven't the slightest idea, Abby. He's certainly not one to drop hints."

The children didn't want much pizza. What they really wanted was to open their gifts from each other, so Betsy and Abby told them to go ahead.

Abby had gotten Jason an electric basketball game, the basketball being a Ping-Pong ball, and Betsy decided to take it along to Nick's beach house. She would practice a few games with Jason and was sure she'd get proficient enough on it to beat Nick. At that thought she realized how really competitive she was.

Carla and Abby were both enchanted by the box of wigs. Abby's head was small and she was able to fit on the platinum wig, which completely transformed her appearance.

"What do you think, Betsy? Would I have more fun as a blonde?"

"I'm a blonde—I don't think it really helps."

Abby winked at her. "But you're having more fun than anyone I know."

Betsy blushed and looked to see if Jason had heard

that remark. It would be just the kind of thing he'd repeat to Nick at an inopportune moment. Or to his father.

Carla had on the Afro wig. "This is how I want to look, Mother," she announced. "You can make lots of little braids on this."

"*You* can make lots of little braids on it," said Abby.

"But I don't know *how* to braid."

Betsy smiled. "I'll show you how next week, Carla. We'll have lots of time together with you out of school."

"I hope she doesn't drive you berserk," said Abby.

"She couldn't possibly; I find her endlessly entertaining. Also, I have a schedule of museum-going all drawn up."

"See, Mother? Some people find me entertaining," said Carla.

Then Betsy and Abby exchanged gifts. Abby adored the robe, which she instantly put on. Her gift to Betsy was a cocoa-brown satin nightgown with ecru lace trim. Betsy had never owned anything so stunning. "Oh, Abby—it's too beautiful. Where would I ever wear it?"

"You've got to be kidding."

Betsy flushed. "I have my old flannel nightgown packed to take along."

Abby grinned. "Why not save it for New Year's Eve?"

"I love it—it's so beautiful."

"You're not the only one who's going to love it."

"You can wear one of my wigs with it, Betsy," offered Carla, and they both laughed.

Betsy and Jason left early, as Abby was making an early start in the morning. Jason didn't have to ask her twice if she wanted to play the basketball game with him. She played him several games until she felt she knew all the moves well, taking care, though, to let him win, so he wouldn't get tired of playing.

While Jason got ready for bed Betsy packed Jason's things in a small bag and set it beside hers and the two shopping bags filled with presents they were taking along. Nick had shopped for the turkey and the rest of the food, and Betsy had agreed to cook it.

"What am I getting for Christmas, Mom?" Jason asked as she tucked him in.

"You already got your Christmas present," Betsy teased.

"I did not! What did I get?"

"You told me you wanted a cat for Christmas, and you got Blacky."

Jason's eyes narrowed in suspicion. "Then who are all those presents for?"

"Those are for Nick."

"I don't believe you."

Betsy laughed. "You're right, some of them are for you. Let's see, I got you socks and underwear and some new pajamas. . . ."

Jason rolled over in disgust. "All right, I won't ask anymore."

Betsy kissed him good night and turned out the light.

Nick picked them up at nine, carrying down the bags as Betsy struggled with the increasingly heavy cat carrier. At the rate Blacky was going he'd weigh forty pounds by the time he was fully grown. Then he'd really be a guard cat, she thought, chuckling to herself.

The first hour of the drive Jason talked incessantly about his basketball game, not neglecting to mention that he had beat his mother at it every time they played.

"I hope you brought it along," said Nick with a gleam in his eyes as he glanced at Betsy. At that moment she felt rather like a pool hustler.

The second hour Jason listed for Nick every Christmas present he had received in his whole life.

The third hour Betsy talked him into counting VWs again while she and Nick planned what they'd do New Year's weekend.

"There's a couple of parties we can go to if you want," he told her.

"Who's giving them?"

"Pete Beck's giving one, and one of my clients the other."

"No, I don't think so," said Betsy.

"When are you going to stop being paranoid about the office knowing we're seeing each other?"

"Probably never," Betsy admitted.

"One of these days you're going to have to," he muttered.

Betsy moved closer to him, and he put his arm around her. "Couldn't we just stay home New Year's Eve?"

"Absolutely not. Would you like to go to the theater?"

"I don't know."

"Well, we could always go to a club and hear some music."

"I don't care—you decide and surprise me. But no parties!"

"What about New Year's Day?"

She kissed his cheek. "New Year's Day we watch the bowl games."

"Of course."

"In bed," she whispered in his ear.

"That goes without saying," said Nick.

When they arrived at the house Nick and Jason brought in firewood while Betsy put away the food. The snow that had fallen the previous week had all melted in the city, but out there the ground was still covered and the view out the kitchen window looked like a Christmas card.

Betsy hung up their three stockings from the mantel and set the presents out on the coffee table. Jason and Nick were playing the basketball game.

Jason looked up at the presents. "They're supposed to be under the tree, Mom."

"There isn't a tree, Jason." She was a little sorry now that she had told Nick not to bother about a tree. Christmas didn't seem like Christmas without one.

"I have a fake one down in the basement somewhere," said Nick.

"Yeah, get it," said Jason. "I can help you put it up."

They finished their game first, and Betsy was sorry to see that Nick had gotten the hang of it quickly. She wished now she'd had time to practice more.

Jason and Nick assembled the tree and got the lights on while Betsy fixed sandwiches and soup for lunch, then they all unpacked the boxes full of ornaments and tinsel and decorated the tree. Blacky was eyeing it from jumping position on a nearby table, so they pushed it back against the wall.

Jason demanded another game of basketball with Nick, and Nick looked over at Betsy. "Why don't you let me play your mother a game."

"No, it's my Christmas present," said Jason stubbornly.

Nick looked thoughtful for a moment, then glanced at Betsy. "Would it be all right with you if I gave Jason his Christmas present now?"

Betsy nodded. If it meant she could play basketball with Nick, she was all in favor of it.

Nick left the room and came back with a very large box that turned out to be a set of computer games to hook up to the TV.

Jason went beyond being thrilled over the present; he was ecstatic. "Mom, look at this, just what I always wanted." He paused. "But we don't have a television at home, Nick."

"I'm sure Abby will let you hook it up to hers if you share it with Carla," Betsy told him.

Nick, cursing over the complicated directions, finally got the set hooked up to the TV screen, and Jason was soon lost to the world.

"What a great idea," murmured Betsy.

"Yes, I thought so." Nick grinned, sitting down at one end of the basketball game, Betsy took her seat at the other.

This was Betsy's kind of game. It was simple to understand, it took a certain amount of manual dexterity, and you didn't have to think out any moves in advance. She quickly beat him in three successive games and was about to gloat when she saw the expression on his face. She decided not to gloat after all.

"I can only assume you've been practicing," said Nick.

"Jason told you we played last night," she said innocently, "and he beat me every time."

"I saw the way Jason played."

"He was probably letting you win," said Betsy.

"No, Jason's too competitive for that. Rather like his mother."

"You want to try another?"

"I think I've been conned," said Nick.

"Maybe you'll win the next game."

Nick eyed her warily. "How about a game of chess?"

Betsy moved over next to him and kissed him on the side of the neck. "Why don't we go for a walk in the snow, Nick?"

"I don't want to go for a walk in the snow. I want to play you a game of chess."

Betsy gave him a long, lingering kiss on the mouth. His remained stubbornly closed and unresponsive. "Why don't I give *you* your Christmas present now."

"What for?" He sounded suspicious, as well he might.

"Because you'll love it," she said with a sweet smile.

She reached under the tree and handed him the gift-wrapped box. He didn't even read the card, just tore off the wrapping paper and looked at the gift in astonishment. Rather like Jason, she thought.

He looked up at her, a wide smile on his face. "A computer chess set!" He reached out and hugged her. "I love it—I really do."

He read over the directions carefully, then plugged in the set. Soon he was as enthralled as Jason, and Betsy got very bored watching both of them at their games. Eventually she got up, and put on her jacket and boots, and went outside for a walk along the beach.

It was getting dark, and she could see the stars already. The drifts of snow along the sand, the stars, the waves lapping against the shore, all seemed very romantic to her. The only thing missing was Nick.

She went back in the house. Neither looked up from his game; they hadn't even known she was gone!

She went into the kitchen and prepared the stuffing for the turkey. That took a short twenty minutes. She finally found a stack of old magazines and settled down on the couch to read them.

Nick looked up from his game. "This is incredible, Betsy—it doesn't make a mistake! I think it will be months before I beat it."

At least that let her off the hook for months.

"Do *you* want to try it?"

"No, you play, Nick—it's your Christmas present."

"Aren't you bored with nothing to do?"

She admitted she was.

A gleam came into his eyes. "I have a Ping-Pong table in the basement. You want to play?"

Now that was something her brothers invariably beat her at, but maybe Nick wasn't that good. She agreed, and they went down to the basement. Nick straightened the net on the table, then hunted around for the paddles and balls.

"Do you want to put some money on the game?" Nick asked her.

She shook her head. She wasn't going to bet any money until she saw how he played.

Unfortunately he played just like her brothers. He constantly slammed the ball, which she could never return, plus he kept her running from one side of the table to the other while he merely stood in one place. He beat her soundly in several games, by which time she was ready to go back to the couch and read magazines.

Betsy finally put down her paddle and gave up. "Let's play basketball some more," she suggested.

He laughed, then circled the table and took her in his arms. "If Jason wasn't here, we could go to the one place where we're not competitive," he said softly.

She put her head against his chest. "What time is it?"

Nick looked at his watch. "Only five. Not nearly time for him to go to bed."

"Maybe we could tell him we're taking a nap," suggested Betsy.

"I guess mothers are as devious as lawyers." Nick grinned.

Jason didn't even miss them; he was too engrossed in his games.

That night, after Jason finally went to bed, Nick sat down in front of the television set and started playing with Jason's computer games.

Out of boredom, Betsy tried to play against his chess set. She found out something very quickly. It had eight levels, and on the lower levels it beat her very fast, all the lights on the board flashing on and off when it did so, annoying the hell out of her. But when she tried it just for fun on the highest level, the strangest thing happened. Her unorthodox moves seemed to confuse its little computer mind and suddenly all the lights on the board just went out and stayed out. And the game wasn't even over.

"Come here a minute, Nick," said Betsy. "I think I broke your game."

He was immediately by her side. "What happened?"

"I was playing it on level eight and all of a sudden it just quit working."

He looked down at the board, then up at her. "It conceded the game to you. You beat it, Betsy, on the highest level! The 'chess master' level." He was looking at her with something like awe on his face.

"Oh," said Betsy, assuming a nonchalance she

wasn't feeling. However it happened, she thought with relief, he would probably never ask her to play chess with him again. "Want to play some basketball?"

"No," said Nick, "I want to go to bed."

"About time," muttered Betsy, getting up and turning off the tree.

It seemed like they had only gotten to sleep when Jason was outside the bedroom door shouting "Merry Christmas." Betsy got up and went downstairs to make coffee and give Jason a glass of orange juice. Then they settled down in the living room to watch him open his presents.

Although it wasn't as exciting as Nick's gift, he liked the football game, especially when Betsy pointed out to him that it was small enough to take with him on the plane. Nick also seemed to like it, and started playing with it while Jason opened the rest of his gifts. There were some clothes, but they all had writing on them so he didn't mind. Also books and games and lots of chocolate-covered marshmallow Santa Clauses.

After that Nick told them to get dressed, because Betsy's present was outside.

"In the snow?" asked Jason.

"Not exactly," said Nick with a mysterious air.

Betsy couldn't imagine why her present was outside. She started listing outdoor games in her mind but couldn't come up with anything he might have gotten her.

When he finally led them out to the garage and pointed it out to her, she couldn't believe her eyes. It was a bright red motor scooter, and she couldn't have been more excited.

"Oh, Nick—oh, it's too much, Nick, you shouldn't have gotten me that—oh, but I love it so much. How did you think of it? How did you ever think of it?"

"That's the neatest gift I ever saw," breathed Jason, his eyes as wide as his mother's. "You sure give neat gifts, Nick."

"I thought you might have fun on it," said Nick modestly.

"How are we going to get it home?" asked Jason.

"I'm going to ride it," said Betsy.

Nick shook his head. "No, you're not. I got it out here in my trunk, I can get it back that way."

"But I want to ride it home!" wailed Betsy.

"No way—but you can take us for a ride on it now."

Betsy took them each for a ride on it, loving the way it handled. Then Nick wanted a turn, and Betsy gave in gracefully. After that Jason wanted a turn, but they both said no.

The dinner turned out delicious. "I can ride you to the airport on my scooter tomorrow," Betsy told Jason.

"No," said Nick. "I'll take off work and drive him there."

"What's the point of buying it for me if I can't ride it anywhere?" She was gnawing on a turkey leg, which rather slurred her words.

"I'd rather you just rode it around the city," said Nick.

Which is exactly what she did the following week, but Nick did take off work to drive her and Jason to the airport. Jason was very excited about riding on the plane alone. Despite the fact that he carried his football game and two books on the plane with him, Betsy was sure his seat partner would be talked to death the entire flight. Jason always treated strangers like old friends.

It was cold but clear the week after Christmas, and Betsy and Carla spent their days riding all over the city on the motor scooter. The super was agreeable to her keeping it under the stairs in the entry hall for an additional twenty-five dollars a month, which she was sure he slipped right into his own pocket. It was worth it, though. She could get to places in the city now where it had been too far for her to walk before. She and Carla rode as far north as the Cloisters to view the famous unicorn tapestries and their Christmas tree decorated with antique angels, south to the very tip of Manhattan, where they could see the Statue of Liberty out in the harbor, and one day they crossed the bridge and walked around Brooklyn Heights to see the quaint old buildings and little shops. It reminded her of Greenwich Village, but without all the students.

Betsy was so happy, she wanted everyone to be just as happy, so when Abby told her she had a date New Year's Eve with Gregor, her yoga instructor, Betsy was pleased as could be. When Jason had started playing handball with Nick on Tuesday and Thursday evenings, Abby had signed up for a yoga class to which she could take Carla. Betsy had heard about

Gregor, of course. How he didn't smoke or drink, ate only health foods, and was "physically fit to a revolting degree," but it hadn't looked as though his teachings were having any visible effect on Abby, who stuck to all her old, bad habits. She had a feeling that Abby would turn out to have more of an effect on Gregor than the other way around.

Betsy decided to wear her new outfit on New Year's Eve, no matter where they were going. After all, she hadn't gotten to wear it for very long, and it looked festive for the occasion.

Nick picked her up in his car, which surprised her, as he didn't often use it around the city because of the parking problem. She had her new nightgown and a change of clothes in a bag with her and put it in the backseat. He gave her a kiss, refused to tell her where they were going, and Betsy was completely mystified when he drove out of the city.

"This isn't the way to your beach house," she finally said.

"We're not going to my beach house. And why are you sitting way over there? Come over next to me."

Betsy moved beside him, and he put his arm around her. "If there's one thing I know about you," he said, "it's that you're a gamester. So I decided to take you to where all the other gamesters will be."

"I hope we're not going to a chess tournament," grumbled Betsy.

He chuckled. "No, but that's not a bad idea. We're going to Atlantic City."

Betsy looked at him with excitement. "To the casinos?"

He nodded.

"But I don't have any money with me!"

"I'll stake you to a hundred dollars; after that, you're on your own."

"Oh, Nick—I've always wanted to go to a gambling casino."

"Never been to Vegas?"

"I've never been *anywhere*."

"We'll have to change that, won't we?" he murmured.

Betsy adored the elegant gambling casinos. The hundred dollars lasted her for about two hours. She just couldn't resist the temptation of asking for another card in the hopes of making twenty-one, with the result that she practically always went over. At midnight they had a lobster dinner, and afterward Nick played roulette for a while and Betsy fooled around with the slot machines. She was as excited as a child when she carried a purse full of quarters over to show Nick.

The sun was coming up when they got back to his apartment. They got into bed to get a few hours sleep, then spent the next day watching the bowl games in bed and periodically raiding his refrigerator.

At one point, feeling totally blissful, Betsy had said to Nick, "You know, single life is really fun."

He had smiled and drawn her closer to him. "It's not single life, Betsy, it's who you're with."

Chapter Ten

It was a beautiful clear day with the temperature in the thirties, and Betsy decided to ride her scooter to the airport to meet Jason. She wore her new red crash helmet with a smaller version tied to the back for Jason. Things had been wonderful with Nick in his absence, but now that Jason was returning everything would be perfect. What she liked most of all was to be surrounded by the people she loved.

When his eager little form hurled itself at her through space, his face tanned, his hair tousled, she swept him up in her arms and her happiness was complete. Then a shadow crossed over them, and she looked beyond Jason to see Tom standing there. She could only stand there, speechless with shock, and wonder why in the world Tom had brought Jason back on the plane.

"Hi, Betts, aren't you going to say hello?" He leaned down to kiss her, but she avoided his lips, stepping back and releasing Jason.

"What's that on your head, the latest New York fashion?"

"What are you doing here, Tom?"

"Hey, is that any way to greet your ex?"

"Dad's going to stay with us, Mom."

"Not *with* us," she said, giving Tom a wary look. "Are you here on business?"

Tom gave her his boyish smile, the kind he'd found so successful in the past. "Nope, just came to see you."

She looked at him and couldn't help noticing that he was wearing boots, designer jeans, and had let his hair grow longer. He seemed to have changed his conservative image to that of a swinging single. "Do you have a hotel reservation?"

Jason tugged at her hand. "He can sleep in the other half of my trundle bed, Mom."

Betsy sighed. "All right, but only for tonight. If you're staying longer, you can find a hotel."

"I'm hoping that won't be necessary," said Tom.

Betsy led them out to the parking lot where her scooter was parked. Jason immediately spotted his new helmet and put it on. Tom just stood there looking askance.

"Don't tell me you ride this thing," he demanded to know.

"It's perfectly safe," said Betsy, climbing on.

Tom was looking extremely doubtful. "What about a helmet for me?"

With a look of exasperation, Betsy took off hers and handed it to him. She was even more exasperated when he took it.

"I thought Nick said you shouldn't ride this to the airport," said Jason in all innocence.

"Never mind, Jason," said Betsy.

"Oh, don't worry," said Tom, climbing on behind Jason. "I've been hearing about Nick all week. He sounds like quite a guy."

If Betsy made any reply, it was lost in the roar of the scooter as she started it up. She drove swiftly and expertly back to the city, wishing she could see the expression on Tom's face. He wasn't a coward, but he only felt safe when *he* was in control, which he certainly wasn't at the moment.

Tom looked pale beneath his tan as he got off the scooter outside Betsy's building. She parked the scooter inside, then led the way up the stairs to the apartment.

Jason rushed inside to hug Blacky, then checked over all the Christmas gifts he hadn't been able to take with him.

"I didn't know you had a cat."

"Jason wanted one."

"I'm allergic to cats."

"Yes, I know—but we aren't," Betsy said a little shortly, then instantly felt ashamed of herself. She had lived with the man for ten years. She could really treat him more politely. "Would you like some coffee, Tom?"

"That would just hit the spot," he said, looking around the apartment. "This is a cute little place, but then you always did have a talent for making places homey. Remember that first place we lived in off campus? Emerson Street?"

Betsy hoped she wasn't going to be led by Tom on a nostalgic journey to their past. "Umm," she said in a noncommittal tone.

"Hey, Betts, you remember that Italian restaurant we found on Second Avenue? Great lasagna. How about if I take you to dinner there tonight?"

Betsy remembered it well. It was there that Tom had asked her for a divorce. She had been sure at the time that he chose a public place in which to tell her so she wouldn't create a scene. "I work nights, Tom," she said.

"Oh. Well, couldn't you take off tonight? After all, it's not every night I come to town."

Betsy was about to say no, then reconsidered. If any of her relatives had visited her, she would certainly have taken the night off. She really should do the same for Jason's father, she supposed.

"All right. I'll call and see what the work load's like."

Betsy called the office and asked for Abby. "Listen, Abby, would you cross me out in the night book? I'm going to take a vacation day."

"Big reunion with the kid?" asked Abby.

"Not exactly," said Betsy, "his father's here for the night."

"Wow. Do I get to meet him?"

"You can not only meet him, you can have him as a houseguest," Betsy whispered into the phone.

While they sat and had their coffee Betsy plied Jason with questions about the ski trip, and then it was time to pick up Carla from school.

Jason couldn't wait to play with his computer games on TV again, so they all moved over to Abby's apartment. Tom asked about her baby-sitting arrangements, and Betsy explained to him about Abby.

"Do you think she'd mind watching Jason tonight while I take you out to dinner?"

"She wouldn't mind, but don't you want him along?"

"I've been with him all week, Betsy. What's the matter, you afraid to be alone with me?"

She wasn't afraid, but she found she felt ill at ease around him, as if he were some relative of hers she didn't know very well.

Shortly before Abby arrived home she heard the telephone ringing in her apartment and ran over to answer it. She knew it would be Nick, and it was.

"I know you're never sick, so what's the story? Did Jason get home all right?"

"Yes. But his father came with him."

There was a pause. "Had you expected him?"

"No, and he didn't expect to be driving to the airport on a motor scooter, either."

"I thought I told you not to ride that to the airport."

"I'm an adult, Nick—I'll do what I please."

"Yeah, well I worry about you."

"I'm surprised you even gave it to me. It's just one more thing for you to be paranoid about. Heavens, some mugger on a motor scooter might attack me!"

"Very funny, Betsy. Look, I'll see you tomorrow. Take care."

He hung up before she could say anything. She was sorry she had told him how she had gotten to the airport, as now he sounded mad. If she was working tonight, all she'd have to do would be poke her head in his office and smile at him, and everything would be all right. Tomorrow night they'd make it up. She had enough on her mind tonight with Tom to contend with.

Abby arrived home and agreed to watch Jason.

Betsy could tell that she wasn't too taken with Tom. Tom, however, downright disliked Abby on sight.

"That's a pretty weird friend you have there, Betts," he said when they went back to her apartment for their coats.

"Abby isn't weird at all. She's the best friend I've ever had."

"She looks like a hippy to me."

"Just because she doesn't dress like the country club set you think she's a hippy. You're rather provincial in your views, aren't you?"

"Well, I'm not a big city sophisticate like yourself. And that kid of hers is rather strange-looking, too."

"Carla? What do you mean?"

"Well, that hair of hers..."

Betsy remembered that Carla had insisted on putting her Afro wig on before meeting Tom. She started to laugh.

"What's so funny?"

"That was a wig. I gave it to her for Christmas to play dress-up in."

Tom laughed too, and the tension eased between them. "All right, I'm sorry I criticized your friends. I didn't come all the way here to fight with you."

"Why did you come?"

"I'll tell you at the restaurant."

They both ordered lasagna, and Tom insisted they have red wine with their meal, although Betsy had never known him to drink wine before.

They ate dinner without talking, rather like when they had been married, and afterward, over coffee, Betsy finally broke the silence.

"Have you gotten married yet?"

Tom looked a little sheepish. "No, it didn't work out. We're not seeing each other anymore. Not for some time, actually."

Betsy was surprised. She had always thought of Tom, when she thought of him at all, as being remarried.

"What happened?"

He shrugged. "Oh, her husband put a lot of pressure on her and she changed her mind. She decided it wasn't a good thing for her kids to have a broken home."

She remembered that Tom hadn't worried about that in the least when he broke up their home. She remembered him saying something about half Jason's friends having divorced parents, anyway; that kids were used to it these days.

"I'm sorry to hear that, Tom."

"I made a stupid mistake, that's all. What about you? Any marriage plans?"

Betsy shook her head.

He reached over and put his hand over hers on the table. "I was wondering, Betts, is it too late?"

"Too late?" She slid her hand from beneath his and looked at her watch. It was only a little past eight. "No, it's early, Tom."

"I mean too late for us."

The unexpected meaning of his words finally sunk in. "Yes. It's too late."

"Is it this other guy? Nick?"

"No. It's you. I don't love you anymore."

"I bet you could love me again. It'd be just like old times. We can buy another house in Glenview—"

Betsy shook her head. "I'd never go back to that old life again. I'm going back to school, Tom; I want to live my own life."

"I don't mind your going back to school again. You know what would be an even better idea? We could have another kid."

Betsy had a feeling it was going to be a very long evening. "I'm sorry, Tom; I'm just not interested. Not at all."

"What about Jason? Don't you think he'd like to have his father around?"

Betsy felt an anger rise inside of her. "You didn't think about Jason before, Tom, don't you think it's a little late now? Jason's doing very well."

"Yes, you're right. He seems very happy. And crazy about that Nick."

"He's been a good friend to him."

"And to you?"

"Yes. I love him, Tom, but I fell out of love with you long before I fell in love with him."

She thought she saw tears in his eyes and felt very sorry for him at that moment. She was so happy with Nick, she really did want everyone else to be just as happy. But he would find someone else. He was young, nice-looking, he wouldn't have any trouble.

He changed the subject then and started telling her the Glenview gossip about their old friends and acquaintances. They even discussed the bowl games, but Betsy didn't tell him where she had watched them. She and Tom had never watched football games in bed.

When they got home she made up the extra trundle bed for him, and they both tucked Jason in. She dreaded having to spend the rest of the evening with him, but solved the problem by bringing out the basketball game. She saw after the fourth game that he was ready to quit, so she started letting him win, and he played for another hour.

When it was finally late enough for her to suggest bed, she undressed in the bathroom and wore her robe over her flannel gown when she made up the couch.

"How about a nightcap, Betts," he said, spotting her bottle of brandy in the kitchen.

She didn't think that was a bad idea. She had a feeling she'd have trouble getting to sleep with him in the same apartment.

He set the brandy on the table, and she sat down with him. "That couch looks big enough for two," he said.

"Forget it, Tom."

"Come on, Betts—what's one last time?"

"Absolutely not!"

"I know if I could get you in bed, I'd change your mind," he said smugly.

She did a swift comparison in her mind between Tom and Nick in bed and almost laughed out loud. "I was very bitter about you for a long time, Tom; don't make me bitter again."

"Sorry, Betts," he said, getting up from the table and heading for the bedroom. "I'll be out of your way in the morning."

She recognized his martyr act and decided to ignore it. She put away the brandy, put the glasses in the sink, turned out the lights, and got into bed. She lay awake until she heard his soft snores coming from the bedroom, then finally fell asleep herself.

BY SATURDAY MORNING she was frantic. "But why would he go to Washington for ten days and not tell me?"

Abby reached over and took her hand. "I don't know, kid—who can understand men?"

"I just don't understand it, everything was perfect."

Abby pushed the coffee cake over in front of Betsy. "Have a piece, you'll feel better."

"I'm not hungry."

Abby whistled. "You've really got it bad, haven't you?"

Betsy gave a halfhearted smile. "I didn't see him at the office all week, but he took Jason for handball. But he didn't even call, Abby, to tell me he was going."

"Maybe he didn't have time."

"You don't believe that any more than I do. I know he was angry about my riding the scooter to the airport, but I'm sure he would have gotten over that by the next day."

"Maybe he was jealous about Tom being here."

"Why would he be jealous of Tom?"

Abby spread her hands. "Who knows?"

"Anyway, I told him Tom was here, and he didn't seem to mind. Oh, my God, Abby—maybe my three months are up? Maybe I wasn't any different from the others?"

"It hasn't been that long, has it?"

"I don't think so, but by the time he gets back..."
She couldn't control the tears that sprang unbidden
to her eyes.

"Don't cry, honey, he's not worth it."

"I bet all the others felt just like me. They probably all thought they'd last longer than three months.
But why did he talk about next summer? Why did he
make plans?"

Abby shook her head. "It's really hard to believe.
I could have sworn he felt differently about you. He
sure seemed in love."

"But he made very sure he never used the words!"

Abby got up and poured them some more coffee.
"One good thing, you'll be starting school soon, and
that should help you take your mind off him. Although I still don't believe it's over."

"Why would he buy me such an expensive Christmas gift if he didn't care?"

"Well, that's relative, Betsy. For you it might seem
expensive, but that's a very rich, very successful law
firm, and Nick *is* one of the partners."

"I guess he can afford to be generous when he's
about to cut a woman loose," Betsy said with bitterness. "The others probably got diamond brace-
lets, but since I was 'one of the guys'..."

"Hey, kid, let's go shopping today. All the stores
are having big sales."

Betsy shook her head. "I don't feel like it."

Abby stood up and leaned over her. "Now, you
listen to me, Betsy Miller, you are *not* going to turn
into some kind of hermit again! A broken marriage,
okay, I put up with that for a while. But we're talking

about the end of an affair here, not the end of the world!''

"If I had known it was just going to be an affair, I never would have—''

"Oh, yes you would—you were crazy about him from the start. Now, listen to me—I don't know that it's over, and you don't know that it's over. So I don't want any moping around here. We're going to go shopping, then were going out to dinner, and then we'll take the kids to a movie. One *we* want to see for a change. Do you hear me?''

Betsy nodded. "You're right, Abby; life must go on.''

Abby laughed. "Oh, no—don't start talking like a soap opera heroine.''

THE NEXT WEEK Betsy made an appointment to speak to Dr. Manzer before registering for classes. He remembered her and asked if she had gotten started on her study of Arabic.

She took a pencil and note pad out of her purse and wrote out a few sentences in Arabic, then handed it to him.

He looked at the writing and then at her. "I'm impressed, I really am—of course, I can't read a word of it myself.''

"I'm not sure I pronounce it right, so I've been concentrating on reading and writing it,'' Betsy told him.

He asked her what classes she was signing up for, and when she told him, including one of his, he looked pleased. "But only three?''

"I have to work full time," she explained.

When he asked what she did for a living and she told him, he told her that she could get the same kind of job at NYU and get all her tuition paid for. "It would be quite a substantial savings," he pointed out to her, "and I'm sure our benefits are just as good."

Betsy sat still doing mental arithmetic in her head. That would mean a savings of almost two thousand dollars.

Dr. Manzer was smiling at her. "If you're interested, I could call the employment office for you and find out if they need someone. Would you like me to?"

"If you wouldn't mind," she told him.

He dialed a number and spoke briefly to someone. When he hung up he smiled at her. "Just what I thought, they're desperate for word processors. Go over now, they'll give you a test, and if you pass, they'll hire you on the spot. And you can work nights or days, whichever you prefer."

When Betsy told Abby about it Abby's eyes lit up. "That's really fantastic!"

"Yes, and I'll be working the same hours as now, and I've scheduled my classes so they're all when the kids are in school. I feel guilty about quitting the law firm, though, after they trained me."

"Don't feel guilty, they'll understand. And that way, if you're really not seeing Nick anymore, it'll be safer. I guess it would be miserable having to work with him under those conditions."

"What do you mean *if*? I haven't heard one word from him."

"Well, he is in Washington."

"The last I heard they had telephone service down there!"

Carla came out of the bathroom dressed in jeans, a sweater, and her long platinum-blond wig. She paraded around the room, but Abby didn't say a word.

Betsy looked at her watch, then poured them each another cup of coffee.

"You like the way I look, Mommy?" Carla was standing right at the table now, in front of their eyes.

"Umm, you look very nice," said Abby in an absentminded tone.

"Is that *all* you can say?"

Abby looked her daughter over slowly from head to foot. "Yes, you look fine. Why don't you go see if Jason is ready?"

Carla stamped her foot in frustration. "You mean you're going to let me go to school in this *wig*?"

"If it makes you happy."

"But all the kids will make fun of me!"

"Then why did you put it on?" asked Abby in a reasonable voice.

"Because I thought you'd make me take it off!"

Betsy couldn't control herself anymore and burst out laughing. "For heaven's sake, Abby, tell her to take off the wig before you confuse her so much, she'll end up seeing a child psychiatrist."

Abby fixed her face with a stern expression. "Take off that wig immediately, Carla—it is *not* suitable for school."

Carla smiled, then assumed a sullen air. "Oh, all

right, if I *have* to,'' she said, stamping off to the bathroom.

"I swear, you two are like a comedy team," said Betsy.

Jason came in wearing his new Christmas shirt with Superman on the back. Betsy had been thinking of Nick when she bought it. She didn't like to be reminded and told him to put on his jacket.

"Do I have handball tonight, Mom?"

"No, Jason, Nick's in Washington." She wasn't sure whether he'd ever have handball again, but she hoped so. She didn't want Jason to feel that the men he liked all disappeared from his life because of his mother.

"Oh, that's right. He told me he was going."

Betsy looked at him carefully. "What else did he tell you?"

"What do you mean?"

"Did Nick say anything else to you?"

"Yeah, he told me my return was getting better."

"That's all?"

Jason shrugged. "I don't remember, Mom. He didn't say anything important."

Betsy sighed. It didn't seem right to cross-examine Jason.

Betsy went down to NYU that morning to register, feeling fortunate that she got all the classes she wanted. Then she stopped by the office to see Ms. Peabody in Personnel. The head of Personnel was a stunning blonde in her early forties with a crisp, ivy-league air about her. Betsy had always found her very supportive and this time was no exception.

"When would they like you to start at NYU?"

"As soon as possible," Betsy told her, "but I told them I'd have to give you two weeks' notice."

Ms. Peabody smiled at her. "You could leave the end of the week, if you want. We've hired some new people, and a couple of them are already trained."

"That would be wonderful, if it's really all right," said Betsy. And particularly wonderful because it would mean she'd be gone by the time Nick returned from Washington. If she couldn't see him the way she wanted to see him, she'd rather not see him at all.

Ms. Peabody nodded. "Yes, it's all right. And I want to tell you, Betsy, I think it's wonderful you're going back to school. I always thought you were too bright for this kind of work."

Remembering back to her training period when the word processor had seemed an enigma to her, she wasn't sure she was all that bright.

On Friday the night staff gave her a little going-away party in the kitchen, complete with pizza and beer. They were all enthusiastic about her going back to school, and she found out all of them had completed college before trying to make it in the theater. She hadn't realized she'd been working with such a well-educated group. George asked for her address so he could send her a flyer for a children's theater play he was going to appear in, and Betsy promised to see it. It would be something Carla and Jason would probably enjoy. Christine took her aside and told her she was moving in with the director she had been seeing. She felt a pang of jealousy, but was happy for the girl. Before she left that night, Lisa stopped by and asked her how things were going with Nick.

"That's all over," said Betsy, not wanting to talk about him.

"Three months and out already, hmm? Well, don't feel bad, it's happened to a lot of us."

Betsy thought about that later. Lisa was a good-looking, intelligent, talented young woman. If Nick had done it to her, and others like her, Betsy was a fool to have thought she'd be the exception. She didn't have anything the others didn't have, except perhaps a son. And he had been interested in her before he met Jason. She was just an ordinary ex-housewife trying to make it in the big city. Nick had probably met dozens just like her. He had looks, intelligence, a solid career, respect in the legal community—he could get any woman he wanted. And usually did, she imagined.

She did wonder, though, how she could be so wrong about the only two men in her life. She had trusted twice now; she vowed to never trust again.

Chapter Eleven

A new routine is always difficult to learn at first, and Betsy was glad her job in the history department at NYU was no exception. It took her total concentration for the first couple of weeks, so that while she was at work, at least, she didn't have time to brood about Nick. She found the content of the work more interesting than the legal documents she'd worked on for the law firm, but what she liked best of all were her classes.

The Arabic was difficult, and she was glad she had made a head start on it. Her pronunciation had been all wrong, but this was quickly remedied when she heard it spoken constantly in class. She enjoyed psychology, a requirement she hadn't fulfilled at Northwestern, but her very favorite was the Political Science class with Dr. Manzer. He was a dynamic lecturer who kept the class enthralled, and Betsy found herself reading everything she could find in the library on the subject.

She also enjoyed being around students again and often met classmates for coffee before class. A lot of the young men flirted with her until she finally made it a point to bring up her son in the conversations, and the flirting ceased, and she found herself becoming friends with them, instead.

Her days and evenings were busy, and Abby, who thought she was being subtle about it but wasn't, managed to find things for them to do on weekends. It was only in bed at night that Betsy's thoughts still turned to Nick. She would remember his kisses, his warm body next to hers, the way they had made love, and she would feel such an emptiness inside of her that she wondered how she managed to get through the days. She missed everything about him, even their fights. At times she had an almost overwhelming desire to call him or ride her scooter by his building, but so far she had managed not to do either and she was certain in time the desire would lessen. She knew that if she could have kept on seeing him, she could have loved him forever, but not seeing him, she had to believe she'd get over it someday. She didn't think it was possible for unrequited love not to end sometime, except maybe in old romantic movies. The kind of movies she and Abby now avoided like the plague.

One day, for no reason at all, Jason asked her if they were going to move back to Illinois to be with his father.

Betsy felt perplexed at the question; he had never asked anything like that before. "Why do you ask, Jason?"

"I don't know. Daddy said we might."

She felt anger at Tom for saying such a thing to Jason before even asking her. "When did he say that to you?"

"When we were skiing. You know what, Mom? He promised to take me to California next summer— to Disneyland."

Betsy felt a pang of guilt. Maybe she was depriving her son of something he needed, wanted. If she couldn't have Nick, did it really matter that much?

"Would you like to go back and live with your father?"

"You mean both of us?"

She nodded.

"I don't know. I like you better here. We have fun together, don't we?"

Betsy nodded, close to tears.

"I miss Nick, though. When's he going to come back from Washington?"

Betsy forced back the tears. He was already back, but she hadn't the heart to tell him. "I don't know, honey. Soon, I expect."

"I hope so! I'm going to forget all my handball."

Abby had told her when Nick returned. "I don't get it," she had said. "Nick's biting off everyone's head in the office, you're moping around here. Is this why the big romance broke up? So everyone could be unhappy?"

Betsy had nothing to say to that; she couldn't see any sense to it, either. But then Abby was probably exaggerating to make her feel better. If Nick was dating someone else at the office and walking around with a big smile on his face, she was sure Abby wouldn't mention it.

One Saturday near the end of January Betsy went over to Abby's for coffee. There was a small envelope on the table, and Abby pushed it over to her.

"Here, I got something for you."

Betsy opened it up and took out the ticket. "A ticket to the Knicks game?" She couldn't imagine Abby having something like that in her possession.

"Someone gave it to Gregor, but he's coming over tonight, instead. I thought maybe you'd want to go, being such a sports enthusiast and all."

"I like basketball," said Betsy, "but I don't know whether I want to go alone."

"Oh, go on—it's a shame to waste it. I'll be home tonight, so Jason can be with us."

Betsy shrugged. It really made no difference to her whether she went or not. "Okay, but don't tell Jason where I'm going, or I'm going to have one unhappy child."

"Listen," said Abby with a conspiratorial wink, "I figure if Jason's here with Carla, Gregor and I can have a little privacy in your apartment."

"Sure, I'll be glad to go," said Betsy. "Thanks."

She dressed warm to go out that night. The radio reported that the temperature was dropping to ten degrees, with a wind chill factor of twenty below, which didn't sound too friendly to her. She put layers of clothes on, wrapped a muffler around her face so that just her eyes showed, and set off for Madison Square Garden.

It was a little eerie walking across Thirty-fourth Street at night after all the stores were closed and the streets were deserted, but as soon as she got as far as Macy's she was swept along with crowds of people headed for the Garden.

She bought a hot dog and a beer to take in with her and found that her seat was excellent. It was warm inside the Garden, and after eating the hot dog and drinking the beer, she started to remove some of her layers of clothes so that she wouldn't freeze when she got back outside. She had her heavy sweater over her head when she knocked into the person taking the seat next to hers.

"Sorry," she muttered, then got the sweater off and was staring into the incredulous face of Nick.

He looked as if he had seen a ghost. "What are *you* doing here?" he asked, his voice a growl.

"Abby gave me a ticket," she managed to say. He was wearing some kind of furry coat and looked like a big black bear in it. An *unfriendly* big black bear. She considered putting her clothes back on and leaving, but then decided she had as much right to be there as he did.

"What are *you* doing here?" she added. She really didn't believe in coincidences. Something like this might have occurred in one of her daydreams, but never in real life. And in her daydreams he'd be looking more pleased to see her.

"Abby gave me a ticket, too," he said, a strange expression on his face.

Betsy's mouth fell open. *Oh, no—Abby wouldn't do something that devious, would she? On second thought, she would. Abby would do something* exactly *like that.*

Nick was shaking his head. "I meant what are you doing in New York?"

Betsy frowned. "I *live* in New York. On Thirty-second Street, if you recall."

She watched him light a cigarette, which now

meant he was holding two. He followed her gaze, then put out one on the floor. "But I heard you left," he muttered.

Betsy nodded, as though to a small child. "I left the office, yes."

"I thought you went back to your husband."

Betsy stared at him perplexed.

"I said to Christine that I'd heard you left to go back to your husband, and she said she didn't know you'd ever been married. Then I asked Lisa why you left, and she said in order to get free tuition, so I figured he was going to pay for you to go back to school."

Betsy waited, but no more was forthcoming. "I still don't understand what gave you that idea," she said, not even noticing that the game was about to begin.

Nick opened his mouth to speak, but there was a roar from the crowd as the two teams came on the floor. When it had subsided he spoke. "I got the idea from what Jason said. At the handball court."

"Jason? What did Jason say?" She realized she should have cross-examined her son more closely.

"He said his father wanted you to move back with him and that he'd spent the night at your apartment."

Betsy was nodding her head. "He did. He slept in Jason's trundle bed."

Nick gave a tentative smile. "He did? In the *trundle* bed?"

"Of course. Where did you think he'd sleep?"

"But didn't he ask you to go back with him?"

"I told you a long time ago, Nick, that I'd never go back to him. Even if I wasn't in love with you, I wouldn't." Flustered by what she had inadvertently let slip out, she turned her head to watch the game. If he *dared* to mention it, she'd kill him.

He dared. "What did you say?"

"Nothing," she said, with a great show of following the game; a game that was nothing more than a blur of color in front of her eyes.

He grabbed her by the arm. "Yes, you did—I heard you."

She tried to shrug off his hand, but he wouldn't let go. "Forget it, I didn't mean to say it."

"Maybe you didn't mean to say it, but you meant it, didn't you?"

"She meant it, buddy, now will you shut up?" came an angry voice from behind them.

Nick got halfway out of his seat and turned around, but Betsy pulled him back down by his coat sleeve. "Don't start anything, Nick."

He moved his face so close to hers, she could feel his warm breath on her skin. "I want to hear you say it again," he demanded.

"Well, you're not going to," she retorted. The nerve of him! She had said it once, he had *never* said it, and now he wanted to hear it again. She had forgotten what a truly exasperating man he could be.

He grabbed her hand and pulled her to her feet.

"Hey, down in front," yelled several spectators.

"Come on, we're getting out of here," Nick said gruffly.

"I want to see the game," Betsy insisted stubbornly.

"Go with him, lady," said the man behind her. "That way maybe *we* can see the game."

Betsy was so embarrassed at creating a scene, she grabbed her clothes and followed Nick out. At their exit there was a round of applause. She didn't know whether it was for the game or because they had left.

Once outside, Betsy felt instantly numbed by the cold. Nick hailed a taxi, pushed her ahead of him into the backseat, then gave the driver his address.

"What makes you think I want to go to your apartment?" she asked him, her arms folded across her chest.

"I *know* you want to go to my apartment. You're in love with me," he said smugly.

"You just dump me after three months, just like all the others, and now you expect me to run back the minute you feel like it? Well, *I* don't happen to feel like it!"

He moved close to her. "Come on, Betsy, tell me you love me again. I want to hear it."

She turned her face and looked out the window. He'd have a long wait if he thought he was going to hear that again.

"Please, Betsy? Just say 'I love you, Nick'—just once."

"Go on, lady, tell him," said the cabdriver, his eyes watching them in the rearview mirror. She marveled at the lack of privacy afforded New Yorkers.

"They're only words, Nick, they may not mean anything at all," said Betsy stiffly.

"She's got a point there, Mac," interspersed the driver.

"I don't think so, Betsy. Maybe with some people, but not you, or I'd have heard them before. I figure by the time you get around to saying them they probably mean something."

"What do you mean by the time *I* get around to saying them? I haven't heard you say anything."

"Me?"

"Yes, you. To coin a phrase, I hear the words, Nick, but I don't hear the music."

"Hey, that's real poetic," observed their friend and confidant in the front seat.

"That was *my* line; she stole it," muttered Nick.

"Well?" said Betsy, patiently waiting.

"Hell, anyone who knows me can see I'm in love with you," said Nick with a growl.

"I guess I don't know you then, because I sure can't see it."

"Oh, sure he does, lady, I can tell."

"See?" said Nick. "Even he can tell."

Betsy smiled sweetly. "I'd still like to hear you say it."

There was a breathless silence in the taxi as they all waited. Nothing was said.

They rode the rest of the way in that breathless silence until the cab pulled up in front of Nick's building.

"I'm not going in," Betsy protested.

He dragged her out of the taxi. "Oh, yes you are— we have some talking to do."

"I never get to hear the endings," mourned the taxi driver as Nick paid him.

They kept their distance in the elevator as they rode up to Nick's floor in silence. She huddled in one corner, pulling her coat around her as though in imminent danger. He leaned back in another, a dangerous gleam in his eyes.

Once in the apartment Betsy didn't even bother to take off her coat. She sat down stiffly in a chair patterned of peonies. She was determined to utter not one word until he told her he loved her. Not just alluded to it, but actually told her. It would have to be "I love you, Betsy," or words very similar.

Nick moved slowly around the room. He took off his coat and hung it up, mixed himself a drink, sat down in a green wicker chair with cushions of purple tulips, crossed his legs, and lighted a cigarette. Then, as though telling a bedtime story to a child, he began.

"Once upon a time this gloriously beautiful young woman came to work at our office. When I caught my first glimpse of her I couldn't believe our luck in having obtained her services. I watched her for a while and saw that she seemed remote, cold, unobtainable. She didn't flirt, didn't even socialize with the other employees."

He stopped to take a sip of his drink, his eyes watching her over the rim of the glass. Betsy folded her arms across her chest and gave him an impassive look.

"And so one night I signed up for her time in order to try to get to know her. I learned some things about her very quickly. She didn't date, she wasn't looking for a husband—in short, a veritable man-hater, or so she led me to believe. And yet I sensed—no, more than sensed—I *felt* a spark ignite between us. I was challenged, I was intrigued—in short, I was hooked."

Betsy would have liked to hear the devious machinations of his mind in more detail but knew she wasn't going to get the chance.

"And then, quite by chance one day, I happened to be strolling through Central Park. And what should catch my eyes but this gorgeous creature, this cold, remote, hitherto conservatively dressed female, throwing a sensational touchdown pass and looking very much like a ragamuffin."

He uncrossed his legs, leaned forward with his elbows on his knees, and stared at her. Betsy tried very hard to maintain her poker face. The use of the word *ragamuffin* had almost shattered it.

"It was at that moment, Betsy, that I fell in love with you. And I've remained in love with you every moment since. Even though, my love, you sometimes carry lovable irascibility a little too far."

She felt a chuckle escape her.

"So, I love you Betsy, is that what you wanted to hear? I love you."

"I love you, too," she said breathlessly.

He cocked his head to one side. "Then why aren't you racing cross the room to fling yourself into my arms?"

The corners of her mouth twitched. "I certainly wouldn't want you to think I was behaving like a ragamuffin."

"Come here, ragamuffin."

And then she was across the room in a blur of motion, and he caught her in his arms.

"Oh, Nick, I thought it was all over. I thought my three months were up," she cried.

"Three months? I never said anything to you about three months. With you I always knew it would be forever." His mouth covered her open lips with a deep, demanding kiss, and she felt the now familiar sensations he always aroused in her.

He moved his mouth from her lips to cover her face with kisses, then said softly in her ear, "Couldn't you remove a few of those clothes?"

She stood up and took off her coat, dropping it to the floor along with her muffler. She unzipped her boots and kicked them off, then got back on his lap.

"A few more?" he pleaded softly.

With a tremulous smile she got up again, took off her sweater and both pairs of socks, then looked at him for approval.

"A few more?"

When she was finally standing before him, naked and lush, he picked her up and carried her into the bedroom. He put her down on the bed, and she waited patiently as he got undressed, then reached to draw him close to her eager body.

His lips found hers as they moved together, her breasts brushing languorously against his chest, the matted hair stiffening her nipples and sending waves of heat through her body. And then their hands explored familiar places while the steadily rising tension between them mounted. She cried out his name, cried out her love for him as he did the same, in the deepest moment of love they had ever experienced.

As they were having coffee in bed before she got up to go home, he turned to her. "Why don't you move in with me?" he said casually.

She leaned against him in contentment. "No, I can't do that, Nick."

"Why not?"

Her fingertips traced his lips. "If it was just me, I wouldn't hesitate"—she glanced around—"although I don't feel quite at ease in this decor."

"But not with Jason, hmm?"

She nodded.

"Listen, Betsy, I want you and Jason to be ready to go at ten o'clock tomorrow morning. There's something I want to show you."

"What?"

"It's a surprise."

She got up and started to get dressed. "And no matter how much I try to guess, you're not going to tell me, right?"

He chuckled. "Right. Anyway, you'd never guess."

When she was ready to go, they clung together at the door for a moment, then he told her the taxi was waiting and she'd better leave. "And Betsy?"

"Yes"

"Be sure to thank Abby for me."

Her eyes were glowing. "Oh, don't worry—I certainly will."

JASON FLUNG HIMSELF AT NICK the moment he saw him. "Where've you been, Nick? I've missed you. I had no one to play handball with. Where are we going?"

Nick laughed. "I've been away, but I'm back now. I missed you, too. And where we're going is a surprise."

He turned to Betsy and kissed her. "Good morning, love."

Betsy gave him a quick hug, then got into the car.

She watched carefully out the window as he drove. He wasn't heading for his beach house, he wasn't going in the direction of Atlantic City, he was merely driving west across town. Then he turned north on Broadway.

"Are we going to Times Square?" she asked as all the movie houses came into view.

"No."

"Lincoln Center?" she inquired as they hit Columbus Circle."

"No."

"The American Museum of Natural History?" a little later.

"No."

He turned onto Seventy-ninth Street and headed for the river.

"I've never been over here," said Betsy.

"Good, then it will be a surprise."

"I didn't know there was anything over here."

"Look, Mom," called Jason excitedly. "Boats!"

Then Betsy saw them and stared in surprise. "I didn't know there was a marina in Manhattan. Do you have a boat?"

He didn't say a word, just parked the car, and they all got out. He led them down the dock to a gleaming teakwood houseboat, opened the door, and stood aside as they entered.

"Oh, wow, what a great boat," exclaimed Jason, running around excitedly.

Betsy walked around slowly, looking at everything. There was a full modern kitchen, a very large living area with modern teakwood furniture, a bedroom with a king-size bed and a full bathroom off it, and another smaller bedroom and bath up a spiral staircase of wrought iron. There were even curtains on the windows, rugs on the floor, and lots of built-in bookshelves.

She envied Nick. She had always wanted to live on a boat since her childhood, when her father used to take her sailing on Lake Michigan. And this had so much more room than a sailboat.

Jason was coming down the spiral stairs. "There's a room up there just the right size for me," he announced.

Nick nodded. "It even has its own shower."

"Wow! I'd never have to take a bath!"

Nick nodded in amusement.

"I could jump right off the deck and go swimming. Are you going to live here, Nick?"

"I'm going to live on the boat, yes. But not here."

Betsy felt a sinking sensation in her stomach. Just when everything was finally perfect, did he mean he was *moving*?

"Where are you going to live, Nick?"

Nick ignored Betsy, speaking only to Jason. "I'm

moving down to Washington, D.C. I always thought I'd like to live on a houseboat on the Potomac.''

Jason looked stricken, which was how Betsy felt. "Why are you moving down there?"

"I like it there, Jason. I'm getting my old job back. Washington's a good place to live if you're interested in foreign affairs," he added, studiously avoiding Betsy's eyes.

Jason was looking very downcast. "I'll miss you, Nick."

"You can always come along," he said casually.

Jason's eyes widened. "You mean it? I could live with you on the boat?"

"Well, I don't know, Jason. Your mother doesn't want to live with me."

Jason turned to his mother. "It would be great, Mom—and we could see Nick all the time." He turned to Nick. "What about Blacky, could he come?"

"Of course. He might even get to like me."

"Please, Mom? Could we?"

Betsy stared at Nick until he met her eyes. "Why are you doing this, Nick?" She paused and shook her head. "Jason, why don't you go up and look at that room again while I talk to Nick."

"Sure, Mom," said Jason, climbing the stairs. "Talk her into it, Nick, will you?"

Nick sat down beside her on the couch. "Betsy, it would be great for you down there. The right schools, the right place for your career; I even have some good connections for you when you're ready to find a job."

"No, Nick—I can't. There's no way I'm going to give Tom any means of taking Jason away from me."

Nick looked startled. "How could he do that?"

"The Illinois courts might not take kindly to my living in sin."

"Neither would the United States Government."

She shrugged. "Then it would be just as bad for you."

He put his hand under her chin and turned her face to his. His dark eyes were warm as they looked down at her. And then she heard the words *and* the music. "Betsy, don't you understand? I love you. I want you to marry me."

IT WAS A SUNDAY IN NOVEMBER. Outside the rain was falling, partially blocking out the noise from below. Jason was spending the day at a friend's house, a friend whose mother was also going back to school and with whom Betsy had an arrangement to switch off kids whenever one of them had to study for an exam.

Nick was downstairs, no doubt watching the Redskins game. Betsy tried not to think about that, as she'd much prefer watching football to studying for her exam on the Middle East in the twentieth century. But no one liked studying for exams, she told herself, and aside from that, life was more perfect than she had ever dreamed possible.

All three of them loved living on the boat, and Jason liked riding his bike again to public school. He was even on a city league football team, and Nick was never too busy to go to his games or to coach him on the finer points of football on weekends. For himself, Nick seemed far happier prosecuting cases for the government than he had been helping corporations set up tax shelters.

Betsy had never been more content. She had a loving husband, a happy home life, and Nick was supportive of her embarking on her own life's work. She was in school full time and found both her classes and the political life of Washington stimulating. If there was a flaw in her life, it was that she missed Abby, but they corresponded frequently, talked on the phone occasionally, and Abby and Carla were coming down to Washington over the Thanksgiving weekend.

Nick had already interrupted her studying twice with furtive knocks at the door. The first time was to bring her coffee, which she didn't refuse. The second was to announce that the kickoff was only seconds away. Betsy told him she didn't want to hear about it.

Now, for the third time, there was a knock at the door, then it silently opened, and she looked up to see Nick's face, an all-too-familiar gleam in his eyes.

"It's halftime, honey, do you want to take a break?"

Betsy shook her head, wishing she didn't find his presence so distracting.

He was inside the room now and leaning back against the doorframe. "Do you happen to know what day this is?"

"Yes, it's Sunday. You should be able to tell that by the fact that the football game is on."

He was shaking his head, looking amused. "I mean the date, not the day. It was a year ago today that we first made love."

It came as no surprise to Betsy that Nick was sentimental. He had been the one to insist on a wedding with lots of pictures to remember it by. She smiled. "Are you referring to the day you lured me to your apartment under false pretenses?"

Nick looked affronted. "What do you mean false pretenses? I was really sick. You know I lost my voice."

Betsy chuckled. "I was referring to the emergency work you just had to have delivered to your apartment."

"I never said I didn't have a devious mind."

Betsy pushed the chair back from Jason's desk and stood up. "I guess I could use a break. Want me to fix some sandwiches?"

"That wasn't what I had in mind."

"Nick, I don't want to break my concentration."

He reached out and drew her to him. "Does making love with me interfere with your concentration?"

"Sometimes."

He let go of her. "Only *sometimes*?"

She put her arms around his waist and rested her head on his chest. "Well, most of the time."

He reached down and lifted her chin with his hand, then closed his mouth over hers, kissing her with a passion that the months hadn't abated. "Just *most* of the time?" he asked her softly.

"All of the time," she conceded, lifting her mouth for another kiss. But instead he took her hand and led her down the stairs to the large bed they shared.

They made love slowly to the gentle rhythm of the boat rocking beneath them, both oblivious to the sounds of the game starting again on the television set. When they had finished, he cradled her in his arms, and there was a look of contentment on both their faces.

"Have you ever regretted marrying me?" he asked her, although his voice sounded confident of her answer.

"Ummm. Every morning when you and Jason get up at the crack of dawn and act so damn cheerful."

"But you turn right over and go back to sleep."

"Oh, it's only momentary. What about you? Have you ever regretted it?"

Nick gave her a lazy grin. "Only at times like this, when your insatiable appetites prevent me from watching the second half of a game."

"*My* insatiable appetites?"

"That's what I said."

She made a move to get up, but he held her fast, one hand moving again to her warm breast. "Of course, it's not really an important game. Not a play-off or anything."

"I'm glad to hear that."

He pulled her over on top of him, their bodies molding together. "I thought you would be."

To be published in February,
four more absorbing novels
from

HARLEQUIN
SuperRomance

DANCE-AWAY LOVER by Casey Douglas
Since the tragic accident that had all but ended her
career in ballet, Raine had feared she would never
dance again. Could the challenge from the merciless
choreographer, Brandon du Rivage, erase that fear?

DARK SIDE OF LOVE by Peggy Bechko
In claiming her inheritance – a sprawling ranch in a
remote part of Mexico—Sirena knew she had
accepted a challenge. But she was unprepared for
the antagonism of her adviser, the dark, aristocratic
Ramón Savedel.

LOVE'S SOUND IN SILENCE by Meg Hudson
Midge found herself more than a little intrigued by
the handsome young newspaper publisher, Brian
Vandervelt, and she impulsively committed herself
to a three-month copywriting job on his paper. But
it seemed there was no scaling the private wall Brian
had built around himself.

SWEET TEMPTATION by Shannon Clare
Liza respected the power Christian Chase radiated
in the art world, but how dare he suggest that her
fiancé's religious cross was a fake! Somehow Liza
had to verify its authenticity, even though it meant
travelling to the Middle East—and there she had
little chance to escape from Christian's passionate
pursuit of her . . .

HARLEQUIN *Love Affair*

This month's titles

A MATTER OF TRUST   *Rebecca Flanders*

Lindsey Madison forgets little things like housekeys, pocket money, and to lock her front door at night. When she comes from Iowa to Atlanta to help her uncle in his campaign for a Senate seat, she intends to focus all of her energy on his re-election. Trey Sinclair, often called Washington's most eligible bachelor, wants to be the new senator from Georgia. He has committed himself to the pressures and obligations of a long, hard campaign and a successful term of office. Lindsey and Trey—on opposite sides of a political battle until their undeniable love joins them as one!

THE SAME LAST NAME   *Kathleen Gilles Seidel*

April Peters knew that Christopher Ramsey did not love her when they married. But Christopher's genteel Virginian background dictated that a woman about to have your baby became your wife in a hurry . . . Innocently April believed that Christopher would grow to love her once they were a family, until her baby died at birth and she was propelled into cold, harsh reality. She left Christopher without a trace as to her whereabouts. Six years later as a successful State Forest Ranger April meets Christopher again. In the serene setting of a natural preserve, old passions turn to mature desires too powerful to be controlled!

CITY LIFE, CITY LOVE   *Beverly Sommers*

Raising a child alone in Manhattan wasn't easy for Betsy Miller. But after her divorce she wanted to start afresh. Her night-time job as a secretary in a law office gave Betsy the freedom she longed for. Betsy's life-style was finally her own, until she made a costly error one night at work—and met Nick Creme. As the firm's hottest lawyer, Nick posed the kind of obstacle Betsy could not ignore. And Nick surely demanded all of Betsy's attention. . . .

UNTAMED HEART   *Elda Minger*

Lions and tigers were a part of Samantha Collins's life-style. As a trainer living in Hollywood, Samantha was used to working with exotic animals in lush locales. Her love for large cats and wild beasts brings her to Puerto Rico, when she gets word about a troublesome tiger on a film set. She flies to join the crew immediately—despite the rumours about the skirt-chasing reputation of the movie director, Ryan Fitzgerald. Samantha never expected to have to tame Ryan's savage soul . . .

NOW AND FOREVER   *Sharon McCaffree*

When Jeannie Rasmussen met Paul Raymond for the first time, she knew that he was something special. But as a highly self-sufficient woman, Jeannie had sheltered herself from relationships since becoming a widow twelve years earlier. Jeannie had her son to raise, and did not want to lean on anyone else's resources for support. Paul felt the attraction, too. He knew that with his own two children, Jeannie would think he was only interested in having her around as a surrogate mother. The warmth of two families and the experience of parenting bring Jeannie and Paul together, but the sparks that ignite into flames of passion in the hot Arizona desert bond them as one!

TWICE IN A LIFETIME   *Rebecca Flanders*

Barbara Ellis didn't think so, at least not until she met Kyle Waters. Tall and ruggedly handsome, Kyle's piercing green eyes told Barbara that he was a man who got what he wanted at any cost—both in his work as an architect and in his personal life. She still treasured her dead husband's memory, and did not want to be unfaithful to the only man she had ever loved. At least not until Kyle began to stir an unbridled passion deep within her, one that he met with a fiery desire of his own!

LOVE CHANGES   *Barbara Bretton*

It took Stacey Andersen five years to put the pieces of her life back together after her fiancé walked out. As a successful businesswoman with part ownership in a small computer company, Stacey was satisfied—until Franco Borelli exploded into her peaceful world. Sophisticated and secure, Franco shook her very core, and with burning ecstasy threatened the deepest, darkest secret any woman could ever reveal!

HOSTAGE HEART   *Renee Roszel*

Drew McKenna was on the run. With the threat of her ex-husband returning to their hometown, Drew was glad to have an excuse to flee to Germany to visit with old friends. When she left Los Alamos, New Mexico, however, she never thought that she would almost lose the most precious gift shared by all Americans—her U.S. citizenship. Rolf Erhardt wanted to escape. He didn't care about anything except freedom. When fate brought Drew to his life, Rolf saw his ticket out. Neither Drew nor Rolf realized that their need to be free from past bonds could never match their burning desire for one another!